An Impassioned Redemption

DEFIANT HEARTS NOVELLA

Sydney Jane Baily

cat whisker press
Massachusetts

Published by Cat Whisker Press

Cover: Philip Ré
Book Design: **cat whisker studio**
Editor: Chloe Bearuski

ISBN-13: 978-1957421049

DEDICATION

To Pandora
My iron-willed, independent daughter
Who personifies bravery and loyalty on a daily basis

I love you more than you can ever imagine!

OTHER WORKS

The RAKES ON THE RUN Series

Last Dance in London
Pursued in Paris
Banished to Brighton
Gretna Green by Sunset

The RARE CONFECTIONERY Series

The Duchess of Chocolate
The Toffee Heiress
My Lady Marzipan

The DEFIANT HEARTS Series

An Improper Situation
An Irresistible Temptation
An Inescapable Attraction
An Inconceivable Deception
An Intriguing Proposition
An Impassioned Redemption

The BEASTLY LORDS Series

Lord Despair
Lord Anguish
Lord Vile
Lord Darkness
Lord Misery
Lord Wrath
Eleanor

PRESENTING LADY GUS

A Georgian-Era Novella

ACKNOWLEDGMENTS

Sincere thanks to the following: My dear friend and fellow writer Marliss Melton, who gave this story the once-over, offering me invaluable advice on personality types. Fellow writer E. Ayers, who generously gave of her time to read my story and steer me in the right direction. Wendie Grogan, who caught typos, inconsistencies, and some poor word choices. This book was made better by all of you.

A NOTE FROM THE AUTHOR

Dear Reader,

While all of my books' heroines are either independent or feisty or unorthodox (or all three), I've never before written about such a wayward female as *An Impassioned Redemption*'s Josephine Holland. Though unmarried, she is not a virgin and is unapologetic about that fact. She is passionate, smart, and liberated, particularly for a woman in the 1880s, and a capable businesswoman, as well.

She captured my interest and my heart when she arrived full-blown and sassy in *An Inescapable Attraction*, Book 3 of my Defiant Hearts series. Though she had only a small role to play, she played it larger than life, helping her friend Thaddeus Sanborn rescue the love of his life, Eliza Prentice. But could a saloon owner who is also a brothel madam have a romantic story of her own? Yes!

Jameson Carter never had a name in Book 3, though he behaved heroically, saving the lives of Eliza and Thaddeus after a terrible shootout. And he lived only a stone's throw away (actually, a river's width) from Miss Josephine Holland. Naturally, this sexy riverboat gambler frequented her saloon. However, he wanted to know her better—intimately, in fact. It was up to me to make his wish come true. This is their story.

Happy reading!
Sydney Jane Baily

CHAPTER ONE

1889, Keokuk, Iowa

Jameson Carter entered The Pork and Swallow, hoping as always to catch a glimpse of *her*. She was elusive though. The lovely Miss Josephine Holland wasn't a common sight, but then nothing about her was common. With her mane of thick sable hair and slanted green eyes that reminded him of the mouser cat he kept on board his boat, she could have any man she wanted on either side of the Mississippi River.

Occasionally, she sat at a private table, sipping some amber beverage, chatting with one lucky customer whom she'd invited to sit with her. More rarely, she had an accounting ledger in front of her and a focused expression on her exquisite face. Tonight, there was no sign of her.

Jameson took a seat at the bar, gestured for Pete to pour him a whiskey, and surveyed the room. He saw a familiar face or two, men who sometimes sat in his own establishment, the best gambling riverboat on this stretch of the Mississippi if not the whole damn river. And with that thought, he always said a private thanks to one Eliza Prentice Stoddard Sanborn, who had made it all possible for him. The gutsy lady had given him her dead husband's ring and his boat, and then she'd left with the love of her life.

Knowing what he knew of love, Jameson thought he'd got the better part of the deal.

Tonight, he wanted an unwatered drink and some womanly company. He could get both on his gambling boat docked on the Hamilton side, but he made it a policy not to take any of his own female employees to the comfortable bed in his cabin. Bad for business. Next thing he knew, they'd be putting on airs and lording it over the other ladies whom he employed to entertain the gamblers, to sing and dance, and to generally brighten up the place.

No, it was better to go elsewhere, and The Pork and Swallow was his favorite saloon across the river in Keokuk. The women were young but not too young. They were well-looked after, so they had their teeth, and one didn't risk French pox by getting close to them. They could even chat about the state of affairs or politics, or they could stop talking and do delightful things to a man's body. And there was always the chance of seeing Josephine Holland, who owned the place along with her business partner, Pete Carlisle.

When Pete gestured as to whether Jameson wanted another drink, he nodded. It was clear to him Josephine was the guiding light behind the success of the saloon, and probably only partnered with the bartender because it was safer for a woman to have a man at her side. He knew in his gut there was nothing else between them, just from the way he'd seen them together.

In fact, he'd never seen Josephine take anyone upstairs with her. Not that it was any of his business.

Jo came down the staircase from the second floor that housed her and four other women—*her girls*, as she thought of them. Glancing around her establishment, she faltered to a halt on the last step when her eyes came to rest on the man in black. Carter.

They'd never been formally introduced, but months ago, she'd asked one of her saloon's regulars about him.

Jameson Carter owned the lively riverboat where she'd once spent the night with its previous owner, the late Jack Stoddard. That had been an evening to remember, though not because of Jack. Unfortunately—or fortunately, depending on one's point of view—the man had been as unable to have relations with her as one of the worms in the small but thriving garden to the side of her saloon.

No, it had been memorable because she'd helped out her good friend, Thaddeus, a man with whom she'd considered falling in love. However, after watching him take care of Stoddard's wife and seeing how they looked at one another, Jo realized what she felt for him wasn't love at all. Instead of the pang of a broken heart when Thaddeus had ridden off with Eliza, Jo had felt only the tiniest twinge of foolishness at falling *not* for the man himself, but for the idea of someone rescuing her from her life, such as it was.

After that night, she'd decided she didn't need rescuing anyway. Her life was damn good. No man owned her or could tell her what to do. And her saloon made decent money, however indecently it made it.

Why she didn't simply stroll up to Carter, place her hand on his broad shoulder, and introduce herself, she had no idea. Well, she did actually. He sparked an interest in her that was simply not allowed. An interest for something more!

Of course, she knew she could have him in her bed if she wanted. All her life, she'd been told of her appeal—she was curvaceous in all the right places and had naturally red-tinged lips to which men showed an inordinate amount of interest.

However, at that moment, she found she couldn't put her lips to use to smile or even to speak. She simply didn't know how to approach a man who made her feel something.

Instead, Jo glided quietly toward her private table. She didn't want to speak to Carter in the guise of a saloon owner and The Pork & Swallow's madam because more than anything, she wanted to talk to him as simply a woman and get to know all about him.

Then she wanted to run her fingers through his dark-brown hair and look into his intelligent toffee-colored eyes. But she *was* a saloon owner and madam, and that was that!

Oh, she wanted him in her bed all right—after all he was the essence of dash-fire and sensual appeal. Perhaps it was her years, but lately, she yearned for an interesting man like him in other aspects of her life. Someone to take supper with, to attend a play, to sit with on a sunny afternoon and talk about the day's events, or to read over the local newspaper. And women like her simply didn't get that opportunity, except the bed part, and then only for a night at a time.

No matter how financially rewarding such an arrangement might be, it wasn't what she wanted with Jameson Carter.

With his back still to her, Jo pulled out her chair, which made a thunderous scraping sound that seemed as loud to her ears as a gunshot. She cringed as heads started to turn and Carter looked around.

When another shot rang out, Jo realized it hadn't been her chair making the first noise after all. All hell broke loose.

As her heart leaped into her throat, she dropped to her knees and scrambled under the table. Gunfights were few and far between, especially in her classy establishment. And even then, a broken window was usually the most damage. Everyone knew this wasn't the wild West of twenty years ago, and she'd be cussed if she'd let her place get a bad reputation because some idiot had drunk too much.

Slipping her small derringer out of its ankle holster, she peered over the tabletop. Not much to see after the initial shots—everyone had taken cover as best they could. She glanced to the bar, where Pete's eyes were staring back at her, barely visible over the polished oak counter along with his Purdey double-barreled rifle. Beside him was Carter, who must have jumped over the bar and taken aim next to Pete.

With his revolver jutting out over the counter's edge, one hand on the trigger and the other on the cocked hammer, he presented an image that captivated her for a moment—calm and controlled, with his golden-brown eyes surveying the room. *Yup*, Jo felt as if she had all the support she needed.

She swung her gaze back over the room. Overturned tables hid most of the patrons in the sudden deadly quiet.

"Who the hell is shooting up my place?" Jo demanded into the silence.

No answer at first.

Then all of a sudden, the table closest to her rolled aside and fell flat with a crash. Frank Hirsch stood up, holding one of her girls—Madeleine, a sweet blonde who could do things with her tongue that made her extremely popular. Some nights, however, she was as choosy as a wealthy virgin princess, especially when it came to men like Hirsch, a little heavyset and not very attractive with large chipmunk jowls. For him, the pretty woman would do nothing more than sit on his lap and sell him Pete's good booze.

Jo sized it up in an instant because she knew Frank Hirsch had propositioned Madeleine more than once and had been soundly rebuffed each time. Frank was a strange one, an Evangelical preacher with a bible always tucked in his pocket and usually a glass of whiskey in his hand.

Blazes! If she hadn't been so distracted by Carter, she'd have noticed trouble brewing as soon as she'd entered the room.

"Frank, honey, what in the hell are you doing?" she asked him.

"I want Miss Madeleine to take me upstairs," he said, a slight slur to his voice, and his grip tightened around the young woman's waist, as Madeleine pushed against him trying to free herself. "And no one is going to stop me," Frank added belligerently.

Jo's eyebrows lifted. *Did he think firing his gun would get him what he wanted?* Liquor had obviously turned his brain to mush. It was clear from Madeleine's stricken expression as she squirmed in his arms that she feared Frank's unpredictability.

"No one forces my girls anywhere," Jo said, and knowing she was taking a risk, she slowly stood. Out of the corner of her eye, she watched Pete's head rise higher above the bar, and she even saw Carter shake his head in warning.

"I don't want to force her," Frank said, "I want her to like me." He gave Madeleine a shake to still her movements, and when that didn't stop her struggling, he put his pistol to her ribs.

"Do you want to be banned from The Pork and Swallow?" Jo asked, taking a step away from her table, the derringer all but hidden in her palm.

"No, ma'am," he said. "But I'm sick of her games. I can help her see the light of the gospel and become a good preacher's wife. She just has to submit to me is all."

"Frank, you listen to me and you listen good. You put your gun away and you let Madeleine go. If you don't do it by the time I count to five, you will never be allowed to set foot in here again. One," she started to count.

"I aim to have her," Frank insisted.

"Two," Jo said.

"I've been waitin' long enough."

"Three."

"That's not fair," Frank bellowed. "Stop your damn countin'."

"Four."

Jo felt cold drops of fear slide down her spine. The last thing she wanted was to be saying "five" and have him still holding Madeleine. Then what? She'd have to shoot him or lose all control of the situation, not to mention all authority for the future.

Frank shifted his weight from one leg to the other and drew his gun away from Madeleine.

"I am never taking you upstairs," the blonde hissed, and Frank howled before shooting at the ceiling in his rage.

"Five," Jo yelled bringing his attention back to her. And it came back full force, with Frank leveling his gun directly at her.

The sounds of three shots cracked the air at the same time.

CHAPTER TWO

Jameson leaped over the bar as the reverberations faded, watching as Frank Hirsch hit the floor, blood seeping out from under the man's body. Madeleine started shrieking and crying, but Jameson could see she hadn't been hit. Immediately, she was hauled aside by another of the saloon girls, who wrapped her arms around the pretty blonde and comforted her.

His gut told him instantly that Frank was done for. He and Pete had shot the man at the same time, but who had fired the third shot? Turning toward Josephine, he saw the smoking derringer she was still holding at hip height and realized she'd also fired at the man. No wonder Hirsch had dropped like a stone.

Josephine stood unmoving, transfixed, as she stared at the dying man on her saloon floor. Jameson took a step toward her, not knowing what he was going to do. Perhaps comfort her somehow. At that moment, her gaze shifted to intercept his, and he couldn't tear his eyes from hers. Brilliant green, clear, and unwavering. Then he noticed her mouth—her beautiful, lush mouth—was trembling.

As she stared at him, however, she seemed to collect herself. She blinked, lifted her skirt a couple inches, bent down and stowed her gun in one easy motion that took his glance to her heeled shoes and slender ankles. Then, with only the barest of nods, which he took to be gratitude, she turned on her heel and went back up the stairs, her small feet clattering quickly on the wooden treads.

Back in his stateroom on his boat, Jameson removed his holster and put it on the table beside his bed. Times were quieter at his floating casino since the days when Jack Stoddard ran things. Less dangerous. Nothing more than a few fistfights and, rarely, an occasional shooting over the deck rail spurred by exhilaration if someone won big. Still, he would feel naked without his six-shooter, and thank God he'd had it tonight.

Pete's rifle had nicked Frank Hirsch, rest his tortured soul, in the left arm, and Josephine's bullet had hit him squarely below his collar bone, but Jameson's bullet had gone right into his heart. He shuddered to imagine if Frank had only been wounded and angry, and had fired on Josephine at such close range.

Running a hand over his eyes, he sank down onto his bed. She was so lovely, it nearly hurt him to look at her. And he'd barely had a chance anyway, since she'd disappeared so damn fast without a word. Tomorrow evening, he'd go back and see if she was all right.

Hell! He knew she was all right. Clearly, she was a resilient woman who could take care of herself and her business. But like an itch between his shoulder blades that he couldn't quite reach, he also could not ignore the persistent notion he had to see her again.

As it turned out, he didn't have to wait for the following evening, nor did he have to leave his own boat. Finishing a midday meal the next day with his right-hand man, Ben, whom he trusted with his life and his boat and his business—maybe the only person in the world whom he felt that way about—

Jameson saw Miss Josephine Holland's carriage through the open doors of the main gaming room on the second level.

His heart gave a quick jolt, and he sprang up from his seat to get a better view.

Yup, unmistakably her, in a glamorous buggy festooned in red trim, with her quick little gelding trotting up to his dock and stopping gracefully.

Ben stepped outside onto the deck first. "We're not open yet, ma'am."

Coming to stand beside him, Jameson couldn't help the smile that broke out on his face, merely at seeing this particular woman.

"That's all right," he called out. "Come aboard, Miss Holland, and then come on up."

He watched her alight from her carriage, wishing he'd been closer so he could have taken her hand. As it was, he would have looked foolish running downstairs, across the deck, and down the flat, wide gangplank onto the dock. Instead, he tried not to let his impatience show while he waited, appreciating the view as she walked in her own swaying-gliding way.

Moments later, she boarded his boat and walked out of sight through the main cabin. Then she climbed the interior staircase, and he went inside to greet her as she breached the second-floor gaming room where he stood.

What was that sensation rushing through him at seeing her in the middle of his boat? It was delight, pure and exhilarating.

"Miss Holland," he said. "It's a pleasure to see you again."

Dammit! Was he gushing?

However, she nodded as if his words were entirely expected. And she didn't add how the pleasure was all hers as many people did. No fawning from her. He liked that.

She cocked her head. "You may call me Jo. That's what my friends call me."

"It doesn't seem pretty enough," he said. "Anyway, *are* we friends?" Jameson hoped so. Not too much of a leap from friendship to something more, and his gut told him he needed more.

She kept her gaze firmly on his, her green eyes sparkling as if she knew what she was doing to him, merely by standing on his ship, looking like any man's dream.

"You may have saved my life yesterday. In my book, that makes us friends," she said.

He nodded. "We haven't been formally introduced. I'm Jameson Carter."

"I know." She persisted in her utterly direct way of looking at him. No lowering of her eyelashes, no coyness.

Realizing his manners had escaped him along with any intelligent thought, he asked, "Would you care to take a seat? Perhaps have a drink with me?"

Her mouth quirked in a lovely smile.

"Yes, I believe I will," she said.

However, she bypassed the chair he indicated and sauntered over to his bar. She stood by a stool and waited. Rushing quickly to pull the stool out, he enjoyed watching her settle herself on it, placing her reticule on top of the polished oak counter.

Pausing behind her, he wanted to bend his head and sniff her hair. Instead, he edged behind his bar and studied the bottles.

"What are we drinking to?" she asked, and he decided on fine aged brandy despite the hour, pouring two-fingers' worth in each glass.

He placed hers in front of her, noticing how pretty the shell of her ear was before dropping his gaze to her cleavage, which was even prettier. He swallowed, his mouth suddenly dry, and he remained standing where he was. Somehow, the safety of the solid oak between them seemed like a good idea.

"We're drinking to the hazards of owning a bar and surviving," he said.

She nodded and took a sip. "And to friendship," she added.

"Definitely to friendship." He smiled. "But you didn't have to come all the way here to thank me."

She raised a dark sculpted eyebrow. "No, I didn't. And I haven't thanked you, if you'll recall."

He frowned. "That's true. You haven't. Are you going to?"

She sipped her drink. "I didn't *need* your help, Carter."

He started at the way she addressed him, although he liked the sound of his last name on her tongue. But then, he'd probably like anything of his on her tongue.

"Your aim was good," he admitted, "but it might not have stopped him immediately."

"I don't like killing customers," she said, and he saw an emotion flash over her face. *Remorse,* he reckoned.

"Don't worry," he assured her. "You didn't kill him. Nor did Pete." He downed his drink in one draught before he added, "I did."

"Thank you," she said, and he saw relief on her lovely features. Then she smiled. "There, now I have thanked you."

"You didn't have to. Just so you know. And you didn't have to come here today. Sometime soon, I would have been crossing the river to visit your place." He leaned on his elbows, his empty glass cradled between his hands.

"Why is that?" he asked. "How come I'm the one going over there always?"

"Because The Pork and Swallow has an abundance of enticements," she said, with a hint of amusement in her voice.

"So does my boat," he told her. "Good liquor, fair gambling."

"Women, too," she pointed out in his favor.

He shrugged. "None as pretty as your ladies. Besides, mine don't quite fill the same role as yours."

She lifted both eyebrows. "Really?"

"Truly," he asserted. "Mine keep the gamblers company, help sell a few drinks, soothe sore losers, but only in the public rooms. And they sometimes sing and dance if they've got talent."

"I guess your ship does offer many enticements," she allowed.

"I'm short two ladies at the moment," he confessed. "Do yours ever run off and marry your customers like mine do?"

"No, but I guess that's because, as you say, mine aren't quite like yours. I suppose if your girls entertained men in their rooms as mine do, then men wouldn't ask to marry them."

He couldn't contain a chuckle. "You think the gamblers are marrying my women only for amorous congress?"

She shrugged. "There are worse reasons to marry."

What an unusual woman Josephine was!

"Why don't you come some evening?" he invited her. "As a guest of the house."

A shadow dimmed her perfect features.

"I've been a guest before," she said.

Jameson's gut unexpectedly lurched. He hadn't really wanted to discuss the last time Jo had boarded the boat. It was etched in his brain, though, and probably in the brain of every male who'd been witness to it. He'd been working for Jack Stoddard, simply the man who kept an eye on things, making sure no one became rowdy, tried to cheat the house, or ran out on a debt.

In the upper level gambling room where they were currently drinking, he'd heard her arrival that night long before he'd seen it, remembering how the murmurs began, the heads turned, and then absolute silence.

Miss Josephine Holland had stepped a dainty foot on the rich rug, and it seemed as though the Queen of England had arrived. That is, if the queen wore a tight red dress, cut low and cut high. *Hells bells, she'd been a sight!* Every curve hugged and displayed. Her gorgeous eyes had taken in her throng of admirers. Some stunned male had thrust a drink in her hand, which she'd accepted as her due.

Jameson hadn't been able to take his gaze off of her that night. But she'd had a specific mission, which he only discovered later—to distract everyone on board so her friend could rescue Mrs. Stoddard, who was being held captive by her own estranged husband. And then Josephine had zeroed in on Stoddard, himself.

Jameson had watched this exquisite creature play cards with Jack, sit on his lap, even sing so beautifully everyone had fallen silent again to listen. And then, to his disgust, she'd let Stoddard take her to his stateroom, the very one Jameson now used as his own.

"I can see by your face you recall my last visit." She tilted her head, seemingly waiting for some comment.

He shrugged, trying to relinquish the anger he still felt at the notion of short, round Stoddard lying with her. Jack had a personality that was worse than his looks, both rough and cruel. Apparently, Josephine had had a job to do and had done it superbly. She was a professional after all, and he would do well to remember that rather than putting her on a pedestal.

And Jack was dead, which was a good thing, because at that moment, Jameson could cheerfully strangle him for having touched Jo.

On the other hand, now that he considered her unexpected appearance on his boat, maybe she'd come to thank him in the way of her profession. Maybe she didn't like the fact of how he'd visited a few of her girls but never her, when he went to The Pork and Swallow. Maybe...

"Did you get the full tour of the boat?" he asked.

She frowned. "I don't know. What did you want to show me?"

Was that a solicitation? He walked around the bar and stood in front of her. "Did you see the wheelhouse?"

"This boat never goes anywhere," she said, as if because it was stationary, it wouldn't have a place for piloting.

"But it could," he insisted. "And there's a superb view from the wheelhouse."

"All right," she agreed. "Since the weather is fair."

He didn't take her arm as that seemed too forward. But he couldn't resist putting his hand on the small of her back, the first time he'd ever touched her. It felt damn good, too.

CHAPTER THREE

Jameson Carter's broad palm sent prickly warmth through both her close-fitting jacket and her silk corset, right to her skin. Jo hadn't had a man touch her in a long time. She didn't have to, as the owner of The Pork and Swallow. She didn't have to do anything she didn't want to. And Carter was certainly taking a liberty. But she allowed it.

He might simply be doing the gentlemanly thing, putting his hand on her to guide her. The alternative was he thought her an easy chippie. She hoped not. That would put a rapid end to their new friendship.

She couldn't say what drove her to seek him out on his boat. She definitely didn't like being beholden to anyone, and the night before, when she'd fled abruptly for the sanctuary of her bedroom, she'd been both beholden and somewhat shaken. Used to being in control and in charge, she'd looked after her brothers when they were a young family with only a drunkard for a father. Then she'd looked after herself, eventually making enough money as a seamstress to open her own saloon with Pete.

When it came to Carter, Jo wanted to be on even footing at the very least, not a woman who'd been in need of rescue and certainly not a harlot whose favors he could pay for.

He dropped his hand from her as they approached a narrow door painted in white gloss.

"Just a short ladder," he told her. Sure enough, when he swung open the door, he revealed a space the width of a man's shoulders with a wall and a ladder affixed to it. She could look up the seven rungs and see the wheelhouse above.

"Unusual," she said.

"Ladies first," he replied. She'd ascended many ladders in her life, physically and figuratively, and this didn't bother her. She grabbed the rung near her shoulder and put her heeled foot on the lowest one. She started to climb, and then she gasped.

Carter's hands were steadying her at her waist, and she had a feeling he was going to put them on her rear end as she rose higher. Stopping her upward progress, she looked down at him. He was admiring her backside, and it took him a moment to realize she'd halted her ascent.

Moreover, he had a grin on his handsome face that left no doubt he was enjoying himself.

"I'm perfectly capable of doing this without your assistance," she informed him.

He whipped his hands away from her immediately.

"My apologies," he said, with the grace to look sheepish at being caught touching her gratuitously.

Jo proceeded up into the wheelhouse, all the while wondering if he was trying to get a look under her skirts but not really minding one way or the other. Indeed, the view after she reached the top was good, although not much better than from the deck below. The only difference was she now had a 360-degree vista with barely any obstructions.

With her hands on her hips, she waited for him to join her. It was close quarters, and she was no fool. He stepped off the ladder and practically bumped into her.

"At night," he said, gazing out the windows forward and aft before turning his piercing gaze back upon her, "you can see lights all up and down the river, like stars in the inky blackness."

"Mm," she said, not taking her eyes from his face for one second. "I bet you can see them from the deck below, too."

"Or from my room," he said. "It has big windows."

"I remember," she told him tartly, watching his nostrils flare and his jaw clench. So, he didn't like to think of her with Jack Stoddard. *Good!* She wouldn't like to think he didn't care a whit for her virtue, little as she had left.

Making a half turn, she glanced at the spoked wooden wheel and out the front windows, before she realized what was behind her. At her back, beyond more windows that were set into a half wall, was the uppermost deck. Naturally, it had a perfectly good albeit narrow staircase to the level below. She went out onto the uncovered deck, and Carter followed.

"Why didn't you simply bring me up the stairs?" she asked, strolling to the railing. She thought she knew the answer. No doubt Carter had a mischievous streak.

"Not as much fun," he admitted with a twinkle in his gold-brown eyes.

"Are you toying with me?" she asked bluntly.

He was right at her elbow, leaning close, peering down into the water far below. At her question, he turned to look her in the eye.

"No. I'm not."

Their faces were inches apart.

"Then what *are* you doing?" She held her breath, waiting for his answer.

"I don't think you came all the way across the river to thank me. You could've done that the next time I came to The Pork."

She blinked. *What should she tell him?* Certainly not the truth—that she'd lain awake all night, reliving the shock of how close she'd come to being shot by Frank Hirsch. Her life could have ended without warning, just like that. And with that realization came a sudden yearning to seek out Jameson Carter. Not to thank him, but rather, perhaps, to start something with him.

After all, she was in her mid-twenties, and she wasn't getting any younger. She didn't want to die without falling in love . . . and being loved in return.

But how to approach such a subject, she had no idea.

As it turned out, Jo didn't have to say a word. He lowered his head, and before she could think about it, his lips were on hers, firm, supple, and warm. Her senses leaped with delight for his kiss proved even more pleasing than she'd imagined, and she had quite a fertile imagination.

He tipped his head slightly and fitted his mouth more closely over hers. Unthinkingly, she parted her lips to welcome him, and his tongue slipped between them to stroke hers.

Mm, brandy.

Might as well make the first kiss count. Angling her body toward his, she slipped her hands up his chest and around his neck. It had been a while, but she remembered how it all worked. Lacing her fingers in his soft hair, which she'd fantasized about touching, she kept her mouth locked to his.

Longing swelled in her as his hands slid from her waist, palmed her backside, and pulled her hips against his. Her blood flashed to a boil, her body seemed to hum, and her bones liquefied. His scent, a blend of man and bay rum, filled her nostrils.

I could get used to this, she thought. But at that moment, Carter drew back.

"I'll admit I've wanted to do that for a while," he rasped, his gruff voice raising goosebumps along her thighs and arms.

She couldn't help but smile at his honesty, although she guarded her own overwhelming response. And she held back the confession of how she'd longed for his kiss since the first time she'd become aware of him in her saloon.

"Now what?" she asked, her own voice sounding breathy to her ears. She cocked her head, realizing she was asking herself as much as him.

His eyes darkened, and she knew the instant he'd decided he wanted to lie with her. Of course, he did! *What man didn't?* And it would be so easy to give herself over to the desire swirling between them. But a satisfying coupling, even with a handsome and skilled lover, wasn't enough anymore.

The unexpected thought had made her catch her breath the night before. She wanted something more, something she knew she could never really have. And she wanted it with Carter. What a silly notion, thinking he might view her as someone more than a madam, as a woman worthy of a lasting and loving relationship.

He took hold of her hand and led her to the steps. She allowed him, with a wash of disappointment at his assumption she would be readily willing to have a tumble in the sack. They descended to the second-floor gaming room once again, and she was positive he was going to lead her to his cabin, the same one in which she'd entertained Stoddard.

Yet just when she started to pull from his grasp, he bypassed the narrow hallway leading to the prow of the boat and his stateroom. Instead, Carter headed for the second set of stairs. Puzzled, she let him keep hold of her hand all the way down to the lower-level gaming room, out onto the deck, and across the dock. From there, he escorted her to her carriage.

At first, she didn't know what to say. He seemed to be getting rid of her, but in a very gracious fashion. She ought to feel relief he hadn't attempted to seduce her. And she *was* relieved in a way, although she couldn't deny a tremor of disappointment, as well.

"I thank you for the brandy," she said, taking up the reins and not letting her bafflement show.

"I thank you for the kiss," he answered lightly. "I would like to do it again some time."

That deserved an honest answer.

"I would like that," Jo told him.

He stepped away from her horse and nodded.

"I'll see you soon."

She rode home with a strangely warm and unfamiliar feeling. He hadn't treated her like a whore at all.

Two nights later, Jameson returned to The Pork and Swallow—two endlessly long nights and days. If he'd waited longer than that, any remaining semblance of his sanity was going to take flight, leaving him a distracted, preoccupied shell. However, his anticipation died out and his disappointment grew faster than a prairie fire with a tail-wind when he looked toward Jo's table and found it empty.

What did he expect? For some reason he'd thought, after their impassioned kiss, she would be sitting at her table waiting for him. Foolish, he knew.

Dropping onto a stool at the bar, he let Pete pour him a whiskey. One by one, Jo's girls came over to talk to him, determining if he was there for any of their favors. But he politely turned them all away, keeping an eye on the stairs in the hopes Jo would come down.

At last, Pete leaned an elbow on the bar.

"Miss Josephine isn't here tonight," he drawled in a knowing way.

The bartender's words were like a bucket of cold water, which doused Jameson from head to toe and all parts in between.

He wanted to ask where she was while all sorts of inappropriate thoughts sizzled through his brain. *Did she have regular clientele for whom she made house calls?* He felt foolish to have entertained feelings of fondness for her. After all, she was a madam and, whether he wanted to admit it or not, most likely a harlot, too.

CHAPTER FOUR

Jo awakened to the unmistakable acrid smell of smoke and the insistent tolling of bells. With a gasp of alarm, she inhaled a lungful of smoke, sending her into a fit of coughing. The nearby crackling, growing increasingly louder, suggested a horror that had her scrambling out of her bed with haste. The Pork and Swallow itself was on fire. The bells pealed again and again from outside her window, and she realized that was the sound which had awakened her.

On the street, the shouting of voices intensified. No doubt people were drawn to the spectacle, which meant the fire was serious and could be seen from all over the city. Jo wasn't one to panic, never had been, but she also didn't relish the idea of roasting like a Sunday side of beef. And by God, the fire evidently raged close enough to cause her eyes to water.

Her heart, already racing, seemed to pick up speed as she thought about her saloon and her girls. Coughing, she lit her bedside lamp before grabbing her leather traveling bag from under her bed. She darted here and there, moving quick as a minnow, as she gathered up and stuffed half a dozen things of import into the bag—including a framed photograph, her silver comb, a piece of lace that was her mother's.

With her most cherished possessions safely stowed, Jo lifted her mattress and grabbed the wads of cash she kept there for an emergency, although this wasn't the kind she'd had in mind. She put it all in her bag.

After strapping on her ankle holster and slipping her derringer into it, she tossed on her favorite coat over her soft, cotton nightdress. Then she crossed to the door, but she didn't even need to grasp the knob to know it was burning hot. She could feel the fire's heat right through the painted wood.

Lord help her! That did not bode well.

Backing away, Jo took the two steps to her window and pushed up the sash. She stuck her head out, and from this angle, she could see flames escaping through the main door below and licking up the timber exterior to her right. She could also see her ladies milling about in the street, hopefully not getting in the way of the men who had come to fight the conflagration. With gratitude, she noted they'd brought both the piston pump fire engine and the chemical pump, and of course, the hose wagon. The many horses that had pulled all the equipment filled the road in front of her business, causing chaos.

Hoisting her bag's strap over her shoulder, she climbed onto the trellis attached to the side of the building. *Going down shouldn't be too difficult,* she mused, awfully glad she hadn't planted thorny roses but sassy yellow flowers instead. No doubt their solid black eyes watched with amusement as she clambered over them.

When her feet touched solid ground and helpful hands pulled her away from the building to safety, Jo felt relief course through her veins. However, as quickly as it came, it disappeared, replaced by black despair as she looked back at her beloved establishment ablaze with orange flames. The firefighters worked in unison, trying their darnedest to stop the fire from burning its destructive path up the main staircase. However, in her eyes, clearly it was a lost cause.

Where was Pete? At this hour, most likely tucked safely in bed with his beloved Emily at the other end of Keokuk. Most likely, he didn't yet know about the calamity. Although there was nothing she could do, Jo was glad she'd come home and not stayed at her brother's house in Chicago a moment longer. Better to see this for herself than come home to smoking rubble in the morning.

Some of her girls were weeping, having lost their belongings and their place of employment in one fell swoop. However, not one tear moistened Jo's eyes as she looked at the burgeoning inferno. Instead, a hot wave of anger rolled through her, and she felt like hitting something.

It looked like a lot of money going up in smoke.

It looked like the end of her tidy, profitable business.

It looked like a huge chunk of time was going to be wasted, whether she left town to start over or rebuilt there on the banks of the Mississippi.

She set her bag down at her feet as she watched the fire blow out her bedroom window.

It looked like the loss of the only place that had ever felt like home.

Damnation!

Jameson could hear the alarm bells peeling over and over. The river allowed sounds to travel up and down her swiftly running current and to echo across her from bank to bank. He stood in his wheelhouse and looked across to Keokuk, certain the fire wasn't on his side in Hamilton, despite being unable to see any flames even from his good vantage point.

There were many wooden structures all up and down the river, and there were fires nearly every month between the two towns, mostly small blazes that were easily extinguished. As usual, he was glad his business and his home were on the water, relatively safe.

Only briefly, he considered crossing the bridge to see whose misfortune was causing the alarm that night, but he thought better of it. There would be a crowd of gawkers, for one thing. Regardless, he would consider it more than worth the effort if he could drop in on Jo, but she'd been away the night before and might be again. And like a coward, he didn't really want to find out if that was the case.

He descended to the lower deck and poured himself a whiskey.

Jo sat in Pete's kitchen in the early hours just after dawn. She'd stayed in front of The Pork and Swallow until the last ember died but hadn't had the heart to sift through the ruins for anything left to salvage. She'd paid a man to guard the site and then got her horse and buggy from the nearby livery. She'd felt terrible waking Pete from a sound sleep, but he had to learn the awful truth.

Emily, his plain but sweet wife, brewed good strong coffee and placed a plate of the previous evening's custard tarts in the middle of the polished oak table.

Pete sat heavily in his chair, stunned into silence by Jo's news.

She stared at the mug she held firmly between her fingers but didn't remember picking up. Her eyes flitted to Pete's craggy face, then she sipped the coffee before putting the cup down with a clatter that betrayed her strained nerves.

"So, partner, do we rebuild?" she asked.

Looking at his stricken expression, Jo couldn't be sure of his answer. They'd been in business together for four years, quite by chance, and it had worked profitably for both of them. She'd made a lot more as a saloonkeeper than she'd ever made as a seamstress, and besides the cash she had in her bag, she had a goodly sum safely stowed in the bank.

Pete had easily gone from working at a rundown rum-hole in Hamilton near the railway where she'd first encountered him to being her dependable partner. By happenchance, she'd asked him where the best saloon on either side of the river was.

"Ain't been built yet," he'd said.

"Then let's do so," she'd retorted, and they had.

She'd fallen in a good puddle with Pete. Born and raised in the area, he knew everyone on both the Keokuk and Hamilton sides of the river. Sometimes, Jo thought he was such a well-known and well-liked man he should run for mayor of either town. But he liked bartending. And people had entered their establishment knowing Pete Carlisle was an honest pourer, and they'd stayed for Jo's pretty ladies and fair prices.

"There's another building," he said at last. "The old Sawyer place. Bit bigger than ours."

She knew the one, a few blocks closer to the river on 2nd Street. Lammy Sawyer had run a dry goods store before he up and died with no kin. The place had been empty for two months. *Why the hell couldn't that have burned instead?*

She nodded, trying to imagine The Pork and Swallow anywhere but where it had been. Her heart ached at the thought. She'd loved her saloon and her location. She'd had good clientele, the recent run-in with Frank notwithstanding. That had been an unfortunate aberration. And so was the fire.

Two strokes of terribly bad luck. If she were a superstitious woman, she'd start crossing her fingers and looking over her shoulder.

But she wasn't. She was practical through and through.

"We can go take a look at it, I guess."

"First, we'll see if there's anything left," Pete said. "But not now. You need to get some sleep. Whatever's left at The Pork will wait a few hours."

Pete's wife sat with them, and at that moment, when they were faced with going back to look at the ruins of their bar, Emily patted his big hand. She'd given birth the year before and was hoping for another baby within the next year. They would need steady income to stay afloat.

Her small gesture of comfort unexpectedly brought a prickling feeling to Jo's eyes. Sitting in their kitchen, watching them together, only served as a reminder Jo had no one to rely on but herself, and certainly no one to comfort her. In the end, she was alone. Her business partner could always work elsewhere, but his life partner, Emily, would remain by his side.

She pushed her chair out, determined to banish the ridiculously soppy emotion and get some rest.

"Thank you for letting me stay here," she told them. "I promise it won't be for long." It couldn't be. After all, the spare bed was thin as a leaf, and she already missed her soft rug and pretty wallpaper.

CHAPTER FIVE

Jameson watched a young lady march up the road to his boat. She carried a bag in each hand and, as she got closer, he saw she wore an expression as determined as a mule that had decided not to move. Dropping her bags on his dock, she crossed the wooden planks and boarded his boat without a by-your-leave. He saw Ben stop her on the lower level, and their voices drifted up to him.

"Ma'am," Ben said politely, "may I help you?"

"I'd like to see Mr. Carter. I need a job."

Jameson watched Ben look her over. Dressed as commonplace as an Indianhead penny, she had a fair face from what Jameson could tell, but nothing that would make a man sit up and howl.

Apparently, Ben thought the same thing.

"We're not hiring," he said and started to turn away.

"In any case, I want to see Mr. Carter." Her voice was as resolute as her expression.

After a pause, Ben shrugged. "Suit yourself." He looked up at Jameson with a pained look.

Clearly, his friend didn't want the difficult task of telling her she wasn't pretty enough to be one of their ladies. Jameson couldn't blame him. He called down to them.

"Send her up, Ben."

In a moment, the dimpled, light-haired brunette was entering the upstairs gaming room. She looked more attractive close up, and beneath her high-necked frock, she had some gentle curves and a slender waist.

"How can I help you, ma'am?"

"My name is Lucille Strong," she said, introducing herself, "and I need a job."

"I'm sure Ben told you already we're not hiring. We don't need any more ladies at the moment."

"But I heard that you do. You're short two of them."

Damn but word traveled fast along the river! He frowned and stared at her. He was trying his darndest to picture her dressed for work on his boat.

Knowing he was sizing her up, she gave him a thin-lipped smile that didn't reach her brown eyes, while she batted her eyelashes, long thick ones she clearly had no idea how to use in a come-hither manner. Josephine could give this woman some pointers. That was for certain.

"I can start work immediately," she added. "And I really do need employment." Her voice trembled slightly, and he knew he was in trouble. He hated to disappoint a lady in distress.

"What can you do?" he heard himself ask.

"What can't I do?" she retorted, looking more fierce than friendly.

"I meant to ask, ma'am, can you dance?"

"Of course, I can dance. A Virginia reel or a polka."

He couldn't help the smile that broke out on his face.

"It would be more like a gallop. You know, couples dancing close."

She blushed.

"I could learn, I suppose." Her tone held little enthusiasm.

Jameson crossed his arms. *How could he get rid of her without hurting her feelings?*

"Can you sing?"

Lucille nodded, and her face took on an air of confidence.

"Will you let me hear you?" His gamblers loved to hear a woman sing. It soothed them and raised their spirits when they lost. One of the ladies who'd up and married had been his best singer.

"Yes, I'll sing for you. May I sit?"

In answer, he gestured toward the bar, preceded her there, and pulled out a stool. As she settled herself on the padded seat, he noted her thick woolen hose and granny boots. Nothing to entice a man there.

She cleared her throat. "May I have a glass of water?"

Water! He sighed. Good thing he had nothing else to do but cater to this unwelcome female. Nothing like fix the head upstairs, balance the books, order liquor. Knowing there'd be no water behind the bar—who the hell ordered water if they weren't digging a ditch or laying railroad tracks?—he disappeared through the swinging doors to the galley.

"I got a live one for us, ladies," he said to the three who were sitting at the table, eating sandwiches. He scooped a glass of water from the pot on the stove. "She's about to sing if you want to come listen."

He turned heel and ambled back to Miss Strong, hearing the chairs move and the shuffling feet as his employees followed.

Lucille was fiddling with something in her pocket, but left it when she saw he was followed by the ladies.

"An audience?" she asked, frowning.

He laughed. "If you work for me, this room will be packed with people, mostly men, and the room down below, too. Is that a problem?" He set the glass down beside her on the counter.

She sniffed and sipped her water.

"No," she said at last. "I've sung for a few large congregations in my time."

Darla, one of his long-time ladies, snickered. "Like in a church, darlin'?"

"Why, yes," Lucille said.

Jameson had had about enough.

"Go ahead, Miss Strong. Sing."

She took one more sip and put the glass down. If she was generously endowed and had a heart-shaped face, the men who came to play cards and drink on his ship would appreciate her even if she had a voice like a cat in heat. But Lucille didn't have the luxury of a splendid bosom.

When she opened her mouth, and the first pure note came out, Jameson caught his breath. A minute went by, then another. Her voice was like an angel's, and she sang with no music yet kept him enraptured all the same. And it was a popular song, too, not a hymn, as he'd feared it would be.

As she drew a breath and ended the song, he applauded and was joined by his ladies who'd taken seats to listen. Lucille stayed silent, watching all of them with a sharp gaze.

"Your singing is exquisite," he said, "But you're going to have to dance, too. There's a lot of close holding and swaying," he told her. "You're probably light on your feet. That's good. But most likely you'll have men treading on yours."

"Will they?" Lucille asked. "That sounds as if I have a job."

"It does, doesn't it?" Jameson rubbed a hand across the back of his neck and thought for another moment. "I reckon you do."

She smiled, and this time, a glimmer of pleasure flickered in her brown eyes.

"The dancing's not so bad," another of his ladies offered. "And you'll get slipped a few dollars or even silver coins if you let them hold you close." With that bit of advice, his ladies returned to the kitchen and their lunch.

Jameson watched a mask of disapproval slip over Lucille's face, but as quickly as it came, it disappeared.

"I'll get used to it, I'm sure," she stated, starting to climb down off the stool. As she did so, she hooked her boot heel in the footrest and came stumbling toward him. He caught hold of her and suddenly found her in his arms.

As he looked over her shoulder, he noticed Josephine had entered the gaming room unannounced. At the sight of her, his spirits rose, while his groin tightened and energy sizzled through him. He smiled and, without thinking, winked at her.

Probably the wrong thing to do, he realized almost immediately, given the compromising position he appeared to be in.

Sure enough, Jo pursed her beautiful, red lips, which amazingly seemed to be entirely natural, and gave the woman in his arms the once-over with her intense green gaze. Then she just stood there, arching a shapely eyebrow and silently waiting.

"All right, Miss Strong," Jameson said, righting her on her feet and releasing her. "You have yourself a job."

For an instant, a look of repulsion flitted across her features. Or was it mortification at being clumsy? Then she found her voice.

"And a place to live?" she asked, before glancing over her shoulder as she realized they were being observed.

"This is a friend of mine. Miss Holland," Jameson said, stepping even farther away from Lucille. He would have sworn she flinched as if she knew Jo, but when Jo gave a slight nod, cool as a spring stream, Lucille introduced herself.

"I'm Miss Strong."

Jo barely nodded and said nothing in return, so Lucille turned back to him.

"I just arrived in Hamilton and have no place to live. I heard you have rooms for some of your girls."

He wasn't at all sure he wanted this peculiar woman living on his boat, at least not until he knew more about her. However, he had a cabin free, which she would discover soon enough once she started working there. He might as well bite the bullet.

"Yes, I can give you a room. It'll come out of your pay though, 75 cents a week, including meals," Jameson told her, still distracted by Jo's forbidding presence.

"I thank you kindly," Lucille said, sounding as if she were gritting her teeth on the last word, but she smiled slightly. "I'll go get my things."

"I hope not too many things," Jameson warned. "Rooms on boats are tiny by nature."

Lucille nodded and brushed past Jo, who looked about as welcoming as a stick of dynamite in a blacksmith's shop.

After his new hire left, Jameson gave Jo his most winning smile, but she didn't soften her expression at all.

"To what do I owe this pleasure?" he asked.

"Business, simple as that," she said. "That is, if you're done dallying."

Pretending to be wounded, he placed a hand on his heart.

"I never dally with my employees."

"What do you call having your *employee* in your arms and making silly eyes at her?"

Jameson wanted to do a little victory dance at her tone.

"Why, Miss Holland. You sound as if you care?"

"Don't be ridiculous." She swept the statement away with a wave of her hand. "I have a legitimate business offer to discuss. Interested or not?"

"Interested," he said, and he was. Plus, he didn't want Jo to leave anytime soon. He'd talk to her about knitting if it would get her to stick around.

Just then, Lucille popped back in.

"Where should I put these?" She had her bags with her.

"Hold on," he said to Jo and went outside to the railing. "Ben," he hollered.

His right-hand man appeared on the deck below.

"Show Lucille to Rachel's old cabin." Jameson called down. "Just go down those steps," Jameson told Lucille. "Ben will get you settled."

"Thank you," she said, staring right into his eyes with nothing that resembled gratitude. Puzzlement reverberated through him. *What was going on with Miss Strong?* Still, as long as she crooned for his customers, she could be as odd as she liked.

"You'll be stationed in the lower-deck gaming room tonight. The one right below us. Ask Ben to give you a dress and a feather for your hair." He turned away, making certain she knew their discussion was over.

There was Jo, watching everything carefully.

"Do you have time to talk now?" Jo asked him, her tone still tart.

He gazed at her. What a sight she was, even when annoyed!

"Yup, nothing going on till dusk." Once the boat opened, however, he wouldn't have a moment's peace until the wee hours.

"I took a chance you'd have some time this early in the day. Pete should be here any moment."

"Both of you?" Jameson said. So it really was all business.

"Of course," Jo said. "He's my partner."

"Let's sit down while we wait. Can I get you a drink?" Jameson offered.

"Not this time," she said.

Immediately, memories of their previous encounter and their kiss flooded his brain. He'd barely thought of anything else since, except wanting to do it again.

Before he could pull out a chair for her, she took a seat. He thought she looked different than usual, a little weary, a little worried.

"What's this about?" he asked.

"You heard about the fire, no doubt."

"I heard the bells," he paused, then his heart skipped a beat as the awful truth sank in. "Don't tell me—"

"It was my place," she confirmed.

"God, Jo, I'm sorry." He sank into the chair across from her. "Are you all right?"

"Evidently," she said.

"Anyone hurt?" He thought of her pretty ladies who slept upstairs, and blonde Madeleine whom a man had died over.

"No. We all got out. And Pete lives at home, on the southern side of Keokuk. My ladies were awakened by rapping on their doors around the time the fire started. That's what they told me."

"And you?"

"And I wasn't," she said, narrowing her eyes. "But luckily, the alarm bells woke me. I climbed out my window."

"Damn," he swore softly. "I'm truly sorry. Is the saloon salvageable?"

She shook her head. "We retrieved a few things yesterday. Some glasses, the taps, and an ugly painting that just won't go away."

He liked her dry humor, but he could tell she was hurting. Just then footsteps sounded on the outer stairs, and Pete Carlisle appeared.

Jameson stood and welcomed him to their table, shaking the bartender's hand.

"Sorry about the fire. I just heard." He resumed his seat.

Pete shrugged, flipped a chair around backward and straddled it.

"Bad luck is all. We'd had a good run. Maybe it was our turn."

Jo looked as though she didn't quite agree.

"I hear you have a business proposition for me," Jameson prompted.

Pete looked at Jo, who nodded for him to explain. The man tapped his large fingers on the table while he spoke.

"We plan to reopen but not in the same locale. There's another place in Keokuk we like, but we need an investor."

"I see." Jameson wasn't sure if he wanted the complication that would ensue from getting entangled with Jo's business, right at the time he was trying to get entwined with her in other ways.

"*Need* seems like a strong word," Jo said. "We could probably get it up and running with what money we have, but it would be tight, and we want the new saloon to be as nice as our old place."

Jameson nodded. "So, you want a loan?"

"Yes," said Jo.

"No," said Pete.

Jameson looked from one to the other.

"Glad you two partners agree so easily."

Jo spoke first. "I'd rather have a loan, low interest of course, and not have someone else wanting a share of profits. Once we pay you back, you're done and out of our business. Clean and tidy."

Pete shook his head. "And I'd rather not pay interest on a substantial loan, or we'd have gone straight to the bank. But I'd be willing to cut you in for a share. That way, if and when we profit, you do, too. Besides, you might have some good ideas. You run this place," he added, glancing around the attractive gaming room, "and you know about our kind of business."

Jo made a sound that was pure exasperation.

Jameson got up and walked to the bar. He didn't really want a drink, but he needed a moment to think. Business was business, and he had no real connection to Pete or Jo, except for that persistent tug he felt whenever he thought of her. He poured a finger of whiskey.

"Anyone want anything?"

His two guests declined. They weren't the sorriest creatures he'd ever seen, but rather hangdog, nonetheless. He couldn't imagine how he would feel if his boat burned, taking his livelihood and his home in one fell swoop. *Poor Jo!*

Downing the drink, he walked slowly back to the table.

"I think you both have good points, and I can compromise so you both get what you want. I can give you a loan you can hold off paying back for a year or so until you're showing a good profit. If I needed the money, I wouldn't loan it in the first place. Pay it off like you would if I had a stake in your place. With no interest," he added, hoping he wasn't being a fool merely because he had a hankering for a certain woman.

"In any case, I have enough to do running this place, and I don't need a share in yours."

Jo pursed her lips, and he had a feeling she wasn't thoroughly pleased.

"We don't need charity," she said.

Ah, that was it. Her pride was pricked.

"Just be thankful," Pete advised, pinning his partner with a strained look.

"It's not charity," Jameson insisted. "It's one business owner helping out others. Besides, I've always liked The Pork. Where will I go if you don't rebuild?"

Pete smiled. "Miss Josephine has always made sure to have the prettiest gals."

Jameson winced. He didn't really want Jo thinking of him bedding her ladies right then.

"I was talking about the excellent bar," he corrected. "But speaking of your 'gals,' what will happen to them while you rebuild?"

"Don't suppose you're hiring?" Pete asked.

Jo stood up, and both men shot to their feet to join her.

"Mr. Carter has just hired one more, so I doubt he has room for any of ours," she surmised.

"You're wrong," Jameson said, still wondering if she was jealous over seeing Lucille in his arms. He rather hoped so, despite her having nothing to worry about in that regard. Jo was like a bottle of fine wine—red, of course—delectable, intense, earthy, complex, and naturally, full-bodied. Whereas Lucille was ice water. And even Jo's own ladies couldn't compare to their madam. They were more like good-time moonshine. And he'd never cared for the after-effects of moonshine.

"I need one more lady. But whether she goes back to you when you want her, that'll be her decision. She might like it here better. As you know, the job is a little different."

Pete and Jo exchanged a look, likely contemplating which of their girls would be happy not to have to entertain men in her room.

Jameson shrugged. "Just send me one who can dance and flirt. We're all set with the singing for now."

"That's all right," Pete said. "Even if we lose 'em to your place for now, they'll come back after The Pork is rebuilt. No one is better to work for or with than Miss Josephine."

For the first time that day, Jameson saw her smile.

"That's very kind of you to say, Pete. I think we've taken up enough of Mr. Carter's time." She turned back to him, looking less tense than when she'd walked in. Still, Jameson's fingers itched to rub her shoulders until she relaxed under his ministrations. And then he'd kiss her into a complete frenzy of passion.

She interrupted his thoughts. "I'll send one of my girls over tomorrow." Then she cocked her head.

"We didn't talk numbers, but I imagine you have a fair idea of the sum we'll need to get the carpenters in and the tile layers.

If I draft something up with our lawyer, I can drop it back by here in a day or so."

Jameson nodded. "I was going to say I could come by and pick it up, but I was thinking of Johnson Street. So, where's home for you now?"

"I'm at the Fairview Hotel," she said.

He nodded, glad to have that tidbit of information as to where he could find her. It made him feel better somehow, knowing where she was. He wished he had a spare room he could offer her. *Hell!* He wished he could get her to stay in his cabin, but he knew she would turn him down flat.

Long after they'd gone, he was still considering how easily he'd made them a fool's offer. *Had he been too generous?* Of course. And Ben would have something to say about it, that was for sure, something along the lines of how he'd been persuaded by a lovely face and a bustle, all right.

He walked out onto the deck and down the outer stairs, past the motionless red paddlewheel and onto the dock. He glanced back at his boat, unnamed when Stoddard had her and still unnamed ten months later. Everyone knew it as the place to gamble and be entertained in these parts. Didn't need a name, but sometimes, Jameson pictured something painted in sharp black, maybe outlined in red or gold across her white hull. He just didn't know what.

Then he forgot about his contemplations, as he realized Lucille Strong was watching him through the small, square window of her cabin. Before he could raise a hand to wave or even to read her expression, she turned away.

CHAPTER SIX

Back in her room at the hotel, Jo drew a deep breath and let it out again with a huff. Tension tightened her skin, making it feel a size too small, and she didn't particularly wish to examine why. She knew she ought to return to Carter's riverboat with the legal documents the following day, yet she felt a definite hesitance that set her on edge. He'd been beyond reasonable. Pete was pleased, and the subsequent meeting with the lawyer had been perfectly painless.

So what's eating at me? And then it came to her with a harsh twist in her gut. *I don't want to see that woman in his arms ever again.*

Carter certainly wasn't hers to lay claim to. He'd even bedded one or two of her girls before she became aware of who he was—or rather, of how he affected her—but they were *her* girls. Knowing how absolutely disinterested they were in their gentlemen clients, it hadn't bothered her. Much.

That skinny brunette he'd hired was a different matter. She'd given Jo a strange stare that unnerved her, although of course, Jo had delivered an even better glower right back at her.

She paced the room to walk off the unfamiliar feelings. Then putting her hands on her hips, she shook her head at her own foolishness. She'd been used to seeing Carter on her own terms, on *her* territory. That was all it was. And of course, she'd never seen his hands on a stranger before.

It wasn't jealousy, she decided. She was simply unsettled by her new situation.

Descending to the lobby, Jo procured a piece of hotel stationery from the concierge. In a neat hand, she wrote Carter a note inviting him to come to the Fairview's elegant restaurant mid-morning the next day to look over the lawyer's papers. Then she tried to figure out what to do with herself.

At loose ends with no job and not even a home to tidy, Jo decided it was a good day to replenish her wardrobe lost to the flames, which meant going to every ready-to-wear store on both sides of the river. Then she would pay a call on Pete's wife. Maybe she had some sewing Jo could help with. After all, she'd never been a lady of leisure.

No wonder she was unsettled and tending to flights of fancy regarding her feelings for Jameson Carter. She couldn't wait to start rebuilding The Pork and Swallow.

The next morning, Jo's eyes trekked repeatedly to the clock on the dining room's mantle as the hands moved in excruciatingly small increments toward the time she'd suggested Carter should join her. At last, with half an hour to spare before his arrival, she returned to her room to freshen her appearance.

Regarding herself in the mirror attached to the bureau, Jo applied a touch of color to her lips despite their already-rosy appearance, then brushed her hair out until it shone before twisting it into a chignon. Then she froze with the realization she was taking painstaking measures to look appealing—for *him!*

Did Carter think about that sensual kiss they'd shared, the one she relived whenever she thought of him? Had he preened like a peacock to cross the river and visit with her? Probably the answer to both questions was no.

Slamming the brush down on the top of the bureau, she silently scolded herself. She could never become what she was not, an ordinary woman like the one who'd swayed in his arms the day before. Or like Pete's sweet Emily, content to bake tarts and birth babies.

Minutes later, seated at a table next to the window, Jo gazed outside and spied Carter strolling toward the hotel. Her insides did a quick turn at the sight of his striking countenance. Somehow, he'd become the most handsome man she'd ever laid eyes on, and practically overnight, too.

He disappeared from sight momentarily when he entered the Fairview, then showed up at the restaurant's open double doors, scanning the plushly carpeted room for her. She waved him over to her table and waited while he approached and sat down.

"How are you doing?" he asked, his gaze locked upon her face.

Suddenly, she was glad to have taken the time to arrange her hair and add her signature color to her lips.

"I'm fine. A little bored however," she admitted, surprised by how self-conscious she felt beneath his unwavering regard.

"Nothing worse than a forced respite, I suppose," he drawled.

"Precisely. But by week's end, workmen will be over there fixing up the new place," she said, grabbing onto the neutral topic of business. Otherwise, what would she say that wouldn't reveal her secret yearning where he was concerned?

"Which brings me to this." Jo slid the envelope with the documents across the table to him.

"All business," he noted wryly, but not unkindly.

"I will go plum crazy if I don't have my saloon to run, and soon," she admitted.

"I admire that about you, Jo. Most women would be satisfied getting themselves a husband and having kids."

Jo blinked. *My, but that was rather forward of him.* She didn't know what to say so she said nothing, lowering her lashes to shield her feelings.

Why would he assume a normal home life wouldn't satisfy her? He was correct, but still, it stung a little to know he didn't think of her in terms of someone who could be a wife and mother, even though she'd been thinking those very same thoughts earlier.

"Before you know it," he continued, "you'll be ruling the roost again, I have no doubt." Jameson opened the envelope and started to read.

She seized the opportunity to study his features, taking fascinated note of the tiny scar on his left cheekbone—the relic of a bar brawl, perhaps. The slight cleft in his chin drew her attention to the sensual curve of his lower lip. She had firsthand experience with that lip!

She could have stared at his face for hours, but he looked up suddenly, putting an end to her indulgence.

"Everything seems fine," he said, with the hint of a smile. Reaching out, he took the pen that rested next to her hand, brushing her fingers as he did. He may as well have hit her with a sledgehammer for the way her heart jumped.

Their gazes locked for a moment, and she watched his smile spread and his golden-brown eyes dance. It looked like a challenge. Still, she refused to look away.

Dammit! She was Josephine Holland, not a simpering green girl. She would get her reactions under control if it was the last thing she did.

"Shall we head over to the bank now?" Jo asked him, as her breathing leveled out along with her pulse.

He narrowed his eyes, perhaps sensing her struggle, then he signed the papers.

And that was how she came to be walking along Main Street in the company of Jameson Carter. To her amazement, it wasn't awkward at all, accompanying this man. He told her about a customer who'd nearly fallen overboard the night before, and then made her laugh with another story of an outraged wife who found her husband in the middle of a losing streak.

"I've had to deal with a few outraged wives myself," she admitted, "although obviously they're angry over quite a different vice than gambling."

He nodded. "I suppose you're certain you want to own another saloon and not do something else?"

"Why would I—?"

The shot that reverberated in the air and split the tethering post next to Jo was followed by another one that sent pieces of the window frame beside her flying into the air.

Before she could fathom what was happening, Carter grabbed her around the waist and hauled her into the haberdashery beside them, slamming the door.

"Get down," Jameson shouted, pushing Jo to the floor beside him. His heart hammered in his chest at how closely Jo had come to being snatched from him by an unforeseen bullet and an invisible shooter. "Me? I'm pretty sure those bullets were aimed at you."

"Who in the hell would be shooting at you?" she asked, her voice calm despite their situation.

Jo shook her head, clearly doubting him. "That makes no sense."

He said nothing more but levered himself up on his hands and craned his neck to peer out the shop window. Other pedestrians had ducked for cover, too, but now, everything was quiet. He would never be able to tell which window the shooter had fired from in order to chase him down, but he knew a rush of gratitude—whoever it was had piss-poor aim.

Damnation! He couldn't imagine how he would be feeling if Jo had been shot dead next to him. Then he realized he could imagine it all too easily, and his gut churned. He'd made a living with his gun, protecting people, trains, and shipments before he began working for Stoddard. And now he was a legitimate businessman, he didn't want to go back to that life ever again.

For a moment, he considered whether Jo was right, however, and someone from his past was trying to take him down. If so, they'd failed today.

Looking around, he saw two other women and a man lay sprawled on the varnished planked floor, staring with frightened eyes, and behind the counter, he could hear another woman crying. But Jo hadn't lost her composure. He admired her for that.

"We better hold here for a few minutes." He dropped back down beside her.

"Agreed," she said. "This is one of my favorite new gowns, and I don't fancy having to patch up any bullet holes."

He grinned. She was amazing.

"You don't seem too flustered," she said, her green eyes taking him in with an approving stare. "You had a quick reaction out there."

He considered how much he wanted to tell her.

"I used to be in the security business before I took over the gambling boat."

"A hired gun?" she mused.

He wasn't sure if he saw distaste flutter across her stunning features. He hoped not. He hoped it was merely surprise.

Jameson shrugged. "I guess some would call me that."

"And did you do anything someone asked, as long as they paid you?" Her tone had taken on a slightly harder note.

He had done a few things he wasn't proud of, but he hadn't crossed the line.

"I never killed a man for money if that's what you're asking."

A small smile crooked the corners of her mouth drawing his attention. He wanted to kiss her more than ever, right then. Hunger flared and made his blood boil, nearly causing him to miss her next words.

"Good. I wouldn't like you if you had."

He blinked. *Man alive, he was glad he'd passed that test.* The idea Jo might not like him bothered him a whole hell of a lot more than he had thought it could.

"I'm sick of cowering on this floor," he said. "How about you?"

He stood up slowly, held out his hand, which she grasped, and pulled her up to stand beside him. "Come on. Let's get out of here."

They used the back door to the alley behind the line of businesses and hurried along the narrow way. All the while, he kept ahold of her hand, remaining alert to potential danger.

Even after they had eased inside the bank's brick walls with the armed security guard at the front door, Jameson couldn't help scanning their surroundings for trouble while Jo made the transfer from his account to her and Pete's joint business account.

"What are your plans now?" he asked Jo as he hailed a taxi, not wanting to walk back to the hotel in broad daylight along the same street.

"I'll go see Pete. He'll want to meet with the workmen right away. They prefer to deal with me, but then they don't get as much work done, nor do they give me a fair price." She said it without a trace of malice, just a wry acceptance of how the world worked.

"They're idiots," he said.

"Thank you."

"Jo, will you please be careful? That was a bizarre occurrence to be sure, but it might have been an attempt on your life."

She didn't go pale or appear frightened. "A jealous wife, perhaps," she said so nonchalantly it gave him chills.

"Has that happened before?" he asked.

"Actually, no. However, I can't imagine any other reason anyone would want to kill me. And even then, I only *own* The Pork. I don't service the clients. Wouldn't a wife go after one of my girls?"

He was caught for a moment by her words—she didn't "service" the men who frequented her place. Relief, plain and simple, eased his mind and buoyed his spirits. But then he remembered how she'd accompanied Stoddard to his cabin, to occupy him as a decoy. She might not "work" above stairs in her own saloon, but she did sell her favors when necessary, and the thought plowed him in the gut.

He forced himself to stop the path his thoughts were taking, at least for the time being.

"Maybe someone already has gone after one of your ladies. We should check," he suggested. "

"We?" She arched one of her lovely eyebrows, so perfect he wanted to run his finger over its sensual shape.

"I don't feel comfortable letting you out of my sight, at least for a while." It was true. Every protective instinct he had screamed at him to take care of Josephine Holland . . . as if she were his own.

"After all," he added, providing a more logical excuse for his sudden protectiveness, "if something happens to you, then my money is in jeopardy. I'm not sure Pete can make the same magical success of The Pork and Swallow without you."

Her expression turned almost luminous, making her so appealing he would have willingly overlooked even her servicing clients if she agreed to be his woman. Then she smiled at him.

"All right, Carter. Come with me to see Pete, and then we'll check on my girls. I know where two are living, at any rate.

CHAPTER SEVEN

By the time Jameson closed up the gaming rooms at one in the morning, his uneasiness had yet to fade. His sixth sense, honed to sharpness in his previous profession, whispered to him the shooting earlier that day ought not to be dismissed. However, short of kidnapping Jo and locking her in his cabin, there wasn't anything he could do to protect her. He'd left her at her hotel after extracting a promise she would contact him if she needed anything.

Anything at all! *Like a kiss,* he mused. Holding her hand had been . . . perfect. It had made him feel caring, protective, and excited all at once.

Good lord! He was getting it bad for Miss Holland. *Did he want that?* Or was he simply randy as hell and in need of a fine female? Without Jo's establishment, he would simply have to find other things to hold his attention.

Happily, they'd found her ladies were safe and sound, and one of them, Candace, had come to work for him, filling the last vacancy he had. Luckily, the first two women had known where the others were staying, and none of them had felt they'd been threatened in any way.

And not one of them had stirred his interest or made him feel even the slightest tingle the way simply holding Jo's hand had done.

Damn him if his thoughts hadn't flown right back to Jo again.

"Mr. Carter," a thin voice interrupted his thoughts.

Sitting in a chair in the now-silent second-level gaming room, Jameson was startled out of his brooding, surprised he hadn't even heard Lucille's approach.

Wariness rippled through him. He stood up slowly, taking in her costume, the dress all his female employees wore—a grey and white pin-striped gown trimmed with red ribbon, low-cut and off the shoulders, with plenty of leg showing at the front and white ruffles underneath, and the sweetest bustle at the back.

His gals looked trim, tidy, and sexy as hell. Except for Lucille. The low neckline didn't so much showcase her bosom as display her lack thereof. But the hemline offered a generous view of her slender legs, about as shapely as one could hope for, clad in sheer black stockings. He thanked God for sexy stockings.

"What can I do for you?" he asked, as she approached him with her strangely unwelcoming smile.

She stood stiffly in front of him. "I had to take in the dress here," she put her hands on her waist, "and here," she ran her hands higher, "and I think it fits better now. Don't you?"

"You look fine," he told her. "Did you enjoy your first couple nights?"

"Yes. The other ladies have been kind, and the men are very . . . friendly. And they seem to appreciate my singing." Her brown eyes flickered over him.

"I heard you singing," he admitted. "You were splendid."

She put her head down as if blushing, except she wasn't.

"They started giving me dollars when I sang," she admitted. "I didn't know what else to do, so I tucked them down here." She indicated the shallow valley between her small, pert breasts.

He coughed and cleared his throat.

"Good thinking."

When she only nodded, he added, "I have some work to do." Although clearly she could see he was doing nothing but contemplating the night sky. "Do you need something?"

She paused another instant. "No, Mr. Carter. I was just taking a stroll. Learning the layout of the boat and stretching my legs. It takes a little getting used to, living on the water."

"Good night," he said, wanting her gone.

"Good night," she returned and disappeared as quickly as she'd come. He'd had an idea she was going to tell him something more, as there was clearly a lot going on between her ears. Probably trouble.

For some other man. He had no interest whatsoever. As soon as he was alone, Jo's perfect visage with her intelligent eyes and sensual lips floated once again into his brain. He groaned.

Before he thought twice, he grabbed for a pencil and some paper from behind the bar and scribbled a quick invite:

Please come to my boat as my guest tomorrow night, Miss Holland. Good food and good company.
Sincerely,
Jameson Carter

Then he realized it would have to wait until morning, so he scratched out the words "tomorrow night" and wrote in "tonight." He would ask Ben to get the message across the river in due time in the morning, and then he tilted his head back, closed his eyes, and hoped she would come.

To Jameson's surprise, for he'd been half-certain she would turn him down, Jo arrived in her spiffy carriage around suppertime. Ben, as usual, was out front in the early part of the evening, greeting guests and looking out for signs of potential trouble, the way Jameson used to when it was Stoddard's boat.

Watching Ben help her down from her seat, he saw them exchange some polite words he couldn't hear. Even that innocent touch by his own friend caused a surge in his pulse, as if he was ready to fight for her.

However, Jameson didn't move a muscle. He merely watched as she strolled across the dock and onto his boat like she owned the place. He loved that about her.

Waving down at her from his vantage point on the second-floor deck, he called out with enthusiasm, "Come on up."

Lordy, rein it in man! He sounded like an eager schoolboy. But his heart was already thudding at double time. And when she came up the outer deck steps and walked toward him, he wanted to take her in his arms. Something about her made him feel as if she belonged to him.

"What's that smile for, Carter?" she demanded, visibly fighting back one of her own.

"Because you came," he answered honestly. "Simple as that."

A hint of color bloomed in her cheeks. *Pleasure or indignation?* he wondered.

"You know I have nothing else to do," she retorted tartly. "I was rather a safe bet. Don't you think?"

He allowed a small snake of disappointment to slither through him. So she hadn't eagerly responded to his invitation to be with him but had come out of sheer boredom. *Ah well.*

Looking at her, in her gorgeous sapphire-blue gown and her follow-me-boys curls cascading over one shoulder, he felt his smile grow. Any reason that brought her into his presence, he would take and gratefully, too.

The color in her cheeks deepened.

"If you keep looking at me like that, Carter, people will start to talk."

He chuckled. She was so direct. Deciding to answer her directness with a little of his own, he crossed the last couple of steps between them and, even to his own amazement, took her in his arms.

He was rewarded, and arousingly so, when desire blazed in her eyes, but she pressed her hands against his chest, her reticule dangling from her wrist.

"Carter," she warned, her voice purring low and a little gravelly.

"Jo," he said, keeping his tone playful. And then he kissed her, the briefest sweep of his lips across hers. Because he had to. He had to taste her again. Then he stepped back.

She had the look of a woman who might strike out and slap him, but then her affront faded. Instead, she offered a catlike smile.

"Not nearly as good as the last time," she said, cocking her head to one side, "but it'll do by way of greeting. For now." And she turned away, entering the gaming room ahead of him, her cheeks ablaze with color.

A heady rush of power coursed through his veins. He'd made the indomitable Josephine Holland blush!

And she hadn't told him not to kiss her again. In fact, she'd said *for now*, which of course gave him ideas *for later*.

As he drew up beside her, she was surveying the tables, already nearly full.

"You have a good-sized crowd," she said with a hint of admiration. "Should I start offering gambling at my new saloon?"

"That would make you my competition," he reminded her.

"Are you afraid of a little competition?" she quipped.

He looked into her eyes and saw the clear challenge dancing in their verdant depths.

"Not at all," he replied. "But I'd hate to see you spend *my* money to get a gaming license only to find I have all the best high-spending customers on my side of the river."

She laughed. She actually laughed at him.

"My girls will always be prettier," she tossed back. "They're the icing on top of a sponge cake, the sweet treat that would bring *your* customers to *my* side of the river."

"You may have a point." Some of his ladies had worked for Stoddard for a number of years, and Jameson didn't have the heart to retire them, despite believing a few might be nearly thirty! He sighed. There was a lot to being the boss that he liked and a few things he most certainly didn't.

"In your invitation, you said 'good food'," Jo reminded him. "What are we having? I'm not one of those silly females who eats like a bird."

"No, I didn't expect you were." As a gambling man, he would have bet she had a healthy appetite, and not only for food.

Jo let Jameson lead her to his private table in the spacious cabin at the rear of the boat, and they talked as if old friends while they ate. With the backdrop of the gaming going on close by, she learned about his childhood in Montana and told him about her own in Chicago. She could tell he was impressed with her ingenuity of making the jump from seamstress to saloon owner. And in truth, she was rather glad he'd left behind the extreme danger of being a hired gun to run a riverboat gambling operation.

Two hours went by in the blink of an eye.

"I'm going to powder my nose," she told him.

"Your nose is perfect, as is the rest of you." His glance swept over her and heated her from head to her toe.

"Nonetheless." She stood up, warm from his compliment and went to the ladies' washroom.

A few minutes later, Jo made her way back along the short hallway only to stop dead. In front of her was Lucille Strong, peering through the drawn curtain into the gaming room. At first, Jo figured the girl was simply too timid to go out and handle the gamblers the way she was being paid to do. But then Jo saw something in Lucille's hand and felt the skin on the nape of her neck prickle.

Silently, she waited and watched, just as Lucille was doing.

In another moment, the girl raised her hand, and Jo caught her breath, feeling her heart thump in her chest. *Was that the barrel of a gun?* Perhaps Carter was the target.

Without further hesitation, Jo rushed forward and tackled the girl. They went tumbling through the curtain and onto the soft patterned carpet of the main salon. People gasped and a few screamed as the ladies rolled and knocked over a chair, before crashing into a man's legs where they finally stopped. Jo landed on top, pinning Lucille to the floor by her shoulders.

"Christ!" Jo heard Carter exclaim, and then his hands hauled her off his hapless employee. From her place of restraint, clamped to Carter's side, Jo watched as Ben helped Lucille to her feet. In an instant, the brunette's face crumpled from shock to misery, and then she started crying hysterically.

"What in tarnation is this about?" Carter asked.

Jo looked up at his stern face.

Before she could answer, he turned to the now-hushed crowd gawking at the spectacle.

"It's all right everyone. A free beer per customer," he added, giving a nod to his bartender across the room.

As most of the clientele either sat back down or moved toward the bar, Carter's attention returned to the disheveled women.

"Well?" he prompted.

"She attacked me," Lucille blurted out between high-pitched sobs, "like an animal."

"Jo?" Carter asked, his voice dropping a notch with concern as he looked at her.

She smoothed down her bodice and skirt, making sure everything was in place.

"Your Miss Strong was loitering suspiciously behind the curtain, spying on people, and she may have a gun."

"A gun!" Lucille exclaimed at the same time as Ben, who still stood beside her. "That's absurd," the woman continued, wrenching her elbow free of his grip.

"What were you doing, standing so quietly, watching people?" Jo asked. "And what were you holding?"

Lucille looked at her employer, raising her nose in the air.

"Mr. Carter, do I have to answer her?"

"Yes, you do," he said, grim-faced.

She shot Jo a foul glare before addressing her boss. "I was waiting for the right moment when Mr. Arnold would be walking by. He'd asked for one of the special cigars, and you said not to let everyone know you had them because they would all want one."

"Where is it?" Jo persisted.

"It went flying when you knocked into me," Lucille proclaimed, looking like she might start crying again.

Jo narrowed her eyes at the girl for a moment, then scanned the floor around them. Ben and Jameson did the same while Lucille stood with her arms folded.

"Here," Ben said, stooping and picking up a cigar that was under the table.

Jo had been half-hoping it *was* a pistol, although that would have spelled danger for Carter. Instead, she watched him take the cigar from Ben and then shoot her a doubtful glance.

Letting an exasperated puff of air, she accepted her mistake with a shrug. Better safe than sorry.

"Dammit, Jo, what were you thinking?" Carter's annoyance was etched across his face.

She hadn't been thinking too much at all. Just feeling a few things—a little on edge after being shot at, a smidgen of protectiveness in case Carter was the target, and of course, a healthy dose of fear.

However, she wouldn't say any of that. It made her appear vulnerable, which she despised. Instead, she merely spread her hands in defeat.

"Miss Strong looked suspicious."

"I guess you owe her an apology," Jameson said, as Lucille wiped the last trace of tears from her face. Her makeup was ruined.

Jo supposed he was right, but it stuck in her craw to give it for some reason. Perhaps it was the smug expression creeping over Lucille's face as she eyed her or the dismissive glint in the woman's brown gaze. Jo rolled her eyes.

"I'm sorry you looked suspicious," she managed, watching Lucille's thin-lipped mouth straighten in an annoyed line.

"Perhaps Miss Holland should leave, so everyone knows how we handle trouble," Ben suggested.

"Trouble!" Jo exclaimed. *Good God!* She'd never been declared trouble before. Actually, come to think of it, of course she had! But not in this way.

"I've never been thrown out of anywhere in my life."

"I feel very frightened," Lucille said in a shaky voice looking at Jo, "by you. I would like her to go," she added, turning her glistening eyes to Jameson Carter.

Jo rolled her own eyes. What a weak biddy!

But he sighed, then glanced around the room to see if customers were still watching, along with his other ladies.

"It's probably for the best, Jo, if you leave now. Of course you can come back any time."

When hell freezes over, Jo thought. That's when she would step back on this cursed boat. How dare he invite her and then tell her to leave! Without another word, she turned around and walked away—slowly, gracefully, and with as much dignity as she could muster considering she'd been rolling on the rug a few minutes earlier.

Carter caught up to her by the time she reached her carriage.

"I'm sorry, Jo. It's just . . . I think Ben is right, only for tonight."

"I think that's bullshit," she said, startling him into stepping back as she settled herself on her carriage's padded and upholstered dickey and arranged her skirts. "You should be man enough on your own boat to tell Ben you're in charge and to instruct Lucille to pull herself together. After all, *she* wasn't shot at."

"You tackled the girl!" he reminded her sharply, perhaps smarting from the remark about him not being man enough.

She glanced away, an uncomfortable sheepish feeling creeping up on her. After all, she understood about running a business. He couldn't have women brawling under his gaming tables any more than she could allow fisticuffs at her saloon. But this was not how she'd wanted their evening to end.

Apparently, he felt the same way, for he jumped up on the running board and looked her in the eye.

"I'm sorry." And he looked like he meant it. "Business is business, but I appreciate you were looking out for my best interests. If Lucille had had a gun, then Ben and I would be thanking you right now."

She nodded, hating how foolish she felt. *A goddamn cigar!*

"That's fine. Now, get off my carriage." She wished she didn't sound like a shrew.

"Please don't go away angry." His imploring gaze reached directly into her heart, thawing the last of her resentment.

She took a deep breath to relieve the tightness banding her ribcage. What would she have done in his position? Probably the same thing.

"I'm not angry," she told him. *Not much, anyway.*

"Really?" His face brightened so readily she felt a small smile tug at her lips.

Heartened by that apparently, Carter leaned forward and kissed her. He put his hands to her shoulders to hold her there. Deepening the kiss by slanting his mouth, he touched his tongue to the seam of her lips, and she opened them with a sigh.

At last, when he lifted his head, she took a ragged breath.

"You can't keep doing that," she told him. More than anything, his kisses undermined her self-reliance, making her feel as if she had to have another one to survive.

"Clearly, I can." He grinned.

Her small smile became a broader one.

"What do you *mean* by kissing me like that?" She picked up the reins.

"Mean?" he asked. "Why, I guess I'm showing you that I like you."

Her insides fluttered at his frank disclosure. "And do you kiss everyone you like?"

"No, only you. And I want to get to know you better. Are you interested?"

She paused a moment, gazing into his soft golden-brown eyes that glittered in the light of the dock lamps. *What was his ultimate intention?* She wanted to find out.

"I'm interested." That seemed enough of a confession for the moment, so she put a hand to his strong chest. "Time to disembark, Captain Carter."

He nodded and jumped to the ground.

"Hiyah." She flicked the reins, and her horse started off at a trot that soon became a canter.

That man is dangerous. She'd just told him she wanted to know him better. *What if he wanted one thing from her and that was the end of it?* But perhaps he wanted more.

For the first time, she allowed a seed of hope to plant itself in her heart. A life with Jameson Carter, maybe even living under the same roof.

Possible? *Perhaps.* Desirable? *Yes, definitely yes.*

CHAPTER EIGHT

Jameson didn't know what made him go up to the wheelhouse in the wee hours of the morning. Perhaps it was his incessant ruminating about Jo, which kept him from drifting off to sleep. Even when she wasn't with him, thoughts of her kept him company, so much so he hardly thought of anything, or anyone, else.

The sky was still dark, and a million stars twinkled overhead. When he looked into the water, the stars seemed to be floating on the river as if they'd dropped from heaven to play with the fish.

He let the evening breeze lift his hair, and he turned his face into it, inhaling the tang of the Mississippi. *Could he ask Jo to be his ladylove? Did she want that type of arrangement?* He knew he definitely did.

Now that she'd told him she didn't take any of The Pork and Swallow's customers to her bed, and having seen there was no other man in her life, he would like to fill that position.

A banging sound brought him out of his reverie and directed his full attention to his boat.

"What the hell?" he said aloud.

Looking over the side in the direction he thought the noise had come from, he peered into the dark water. Occasionally, a log or a large branch drifted down river and rammed the hull. Tonight, he couldn't see anything, even with the pale moonlight reflecting on the water, except maybe a dark mass next to his boat.

Crack!

Jameson thought the boat shuddered that time. Quick as a mongoose, he flew down the steps to the second level and then charged down the exterior staircase to the next deck, where he ran to the port side to take another look.

Damn! He could definitely see something now, something big, and it was banging against the side of his boat. Moreover, it was stuck fast. There was no one to ask for assistance. There was only him and the ladies on board. Ben lived on land, as did his bartender.

Grabbing the nearest line from the deck, neatly coiled as all his ropes were, he tied one end to an iron cleat in the flooring. After judging the distance to the water, Jameson secured the rope around his waist about halfway along its length, wishing fervently he had another pair of hands.

Going over the railing, he did his best to lower himself down slowly, but ended up falling most of the way and slicing into the cool water right beside a monstrosity of wood and metal that was scraping its way and banging along the hull.

Fortunately, the destructive object, which turned out to be a small, derelict barge or raft, had already cleared the stern's "bustle"—the bulge below the waterline that prevented debris from jamming the rudder. However, some lines drifting behind the barge had caught on the paddlewheel and were holding the blasted object from drifting away from his boat and farther down river.

The slight wind and current were causing the mass to crash continuously against the hull. With both his boat and the barge bobbing, it was beyond difficult to get the thing loose. Treading water, Jameson worked in the dim light with his pocketknife, feeling the sweat pouring into his eyes. Any moment, he expected to see a hole open up in his beloved boat as the scow banged and scraped at it.

Shit!

At last, he got the slab of wood and metal free. Exhausted, he cut himself free from his tether and pulled himself onto the derelict barge, before shoving it away from the hull of his boat and pushing the whole mess out into the current. After riding it about a hundred feet until the trailing snarl of rope was well clear of his boat and dock, he jumped into the inky water and struck out for shore. Wading up the slippery, muddy bank, he rested only a moment before running back to the dock.

Soaking wet, he crossed over the planks and charged into the main cabin. Going directly below to the ladies' sleeping quarters, he located the one where the scow might have caused damage. He pounded on Darla's door.

"Open up. It's Jameson," he said, and the door was wrenched open a few seconds later.

He pushed past his startled employee and lit the bedside lamp.

"You all right?" he asked. "Anything amiss?" Carefully, he examined the interior of the hull. It looked fine, but it could be compromised.

"Enough noise to wake snakes," Darla answered groggily. "A lot of bumping and scraping got me up about twenty minutes ago."

"We had a collision." He ran his hand over the wood behind her bed and could feel movement, like a loose board or maybe it had splintered. "I don't want you sleeping here until I can have the boat's exterior checked over by a shipwright. I'd hate to spring a leak and ruin your pretty hair. All right?"

She paled, most likely at the thought of sinking to the bottom of the river in her sleep.

"Where shall I go?" She grabbed her robe and slipped it over her shoulders.

None of the other rooms had a second bed, except the one Lucille already occupied.

"Go to my cabin. I won't be able to sleep tonight anyway."

After she left, Jameson returned to the main deck, peering down at the shadowy side of his boat. Even with the barge most likely now floating somewhere near Warsaw, he remained on edge.

Pouring himself a shot of whiskey, he went back up two flights to the wheelhouse. He knew he would spend the rest of the night looking over into the darkness where all was blissfully silent, save for the gentle lapping of the river against the hull. If he'd been asleep in his cabin in the prow, he might never have heard the ruckus or discovered the problem until it was too late to do anything but watch his boat sink.

That was assuming he and his ladies had made it off alive. It wouldn't take much of a hole with a steady leak for them all to be at the bottom of the river.

In the morning, after coffee, he slipped into his cabin to get a change of clothes. Averting his eyes from his bed and the sleeping woman in it, he went to his bureau. Darla wasn't on duty until after lunch, so she might as well sleep. The room was dim with the curtains drawn, and he tried not to look at her in case she was uncovered.

Just as he was leaving, he heard a soft moan that raised the hair on his head. It wasn't the sound of someone in peaceful slumber. He dared a glimpse at his best dancer.

"Christ Almighty!" he exclaimed, seeing a stain of blood that had bloomed and dried on his sheets. *Darla!*

Tossing back the bed clothes, he discovered she was bleeding from her shoulder or high on her chest, he couldn't tell exactly. She'd obviously lost a lot of blood and passed out, but she was still breathing shallowly.

"Hang on, honey," he said and backed out before racing to the galley. Christine, his other long-time employee, was having eggs and salted bacon at a small table between the cookstove and the window.

"Darla's been shot," Jameson exclaimed without preamble.

"What?" Pushing her chair back, she jumped up so quickly she spilled her tea in her haste.

"Go sit with her," he ordered, "and see what you can do to make her comfortable. I'll go fetch the doctor."

She started out the door, making a wrong turn.

"She's in my room," he called to her, and she paused to look back at him.

"No, not that," he said. "We had trouble last night and her room wasn't safe."

"Apparently, yours wasn't either," Christine said and hurried off in the direction of his stateroom.

She was right. Blood drained from his head as her quip hit home. If he'd been in his room as he ought to, he'd have been the one shot. Someone wanted him dead! His thoughts turned immediately to Jo, and his heart stopped on a downstroke.

Good God! Could that same someone be targeting her, also?

CHAPTER NINE

Jo jumped at the fierce rapping on her door. Someone was in an all-fire hurry to see her. The shooter from the other day flashed into her mind as she rose from her chair.

"Who is it?" she asked, hating the feeling she had to be cautious, never having had an ounce of trepidation in her life.

"It's Jameson. Are you all right?"

She opened the door to see a decidedly harried man, shirt untucked, hair disheveled, and his clothing in disarray. Oddly enough, he looked as if he might have bathed in his clothes and allowed them to dry while still wearing them.

"What happened to you?" she asked.

"A helluva night. May I come in?"

She stepped aside and ushered him into her room, closing the door behind her.

"Go on. Have a seat. Tell me about it."

He plunked down on the side of her bed, looking as weary as a hard-ridden horse. She leaned back against her desk, her hands resting on either side of her hips on the oak desktop.

Casting his gaze about, he seemed to hunt for the best place to start.

"First, I think someone deliberately tried to sink my boat," he said.

She gasped at the thought of his beautiful boat under water, not to mention its occupants.

"Then I found one of my ladies had been shot during the night."

"No," she exclaimed. "That's terrible. Is she going to be all right?"

"I don't know yet." He ran a hand over his tired-looking eyes.

Jo frowned. "And you came here to see if I'd met the same fate?"

He nodded.

"Do you think this is related to the previous incident?" she asked.

He nodded again and stretched his neck from side to side.

"Maybe two. Not just us getting shot at but the fire that destroyed The Pork."

She narrowed her eyes. "If you ask me, we have a crazed killer on our hands."

"Not a killer yet. Leastwise, I hope not. The doctor said Darla has a chance to pull through. Not a good one, but a chance."

Jo nodded.

"The bullet was meant for me," he added.

"How so?"

"Darla was in my bed."

Jo's heart seemed to plummet to her feet. She was glad she had the solid desk firmly behind her rear end because his words felt like a punch to her stomach.

"Oh."

She had to ask. "Then how—?"

"Her cabin was near where the boat's hull was compromised. I didn't think it safe for her to sleep there."

"I see."

"You believe me?" he asked with a curious expression, as if he'd expected to have to plead his case.

She had no reason to think he would lie.

"Why not?"

He heaved a sigh, but then he frowned.

"You think the fire at The Pork was deliberate?"

She nodded. "I do. I didn't say anything to Pete. I have no proof, but the kitchen was closed, the girls were asleep. I got in late and checked the lamps myself. No reason for my place to burn."

He nodded.

"It seems an odd coincidence, all this bad luck," she added.

"I agree." Then he yawned broadly.

"As you can see, I'm perfectly well. Why don't you stretch out there and take a nap," she suggested.

"What if someone found me in your room?"

They blinked at each other and then burst out laughing. He slipped off his boots and lay down. In about thirty seconds, Carter was snoring peacefully, not a terrible wood-sawing buzz. In fact, the steady sound was rather soothing, reminding her of the drone of bees on a summer day.

Sitting at the desk again, she returned to her work, making supply lists and trying to determine costs.

In a short time, they'd gone from strangers to acquaintances to dancing on the edge of something much more. And she was a little surprised at how pleased she felt and how she was looking forward to whatever came next. That was, if whoever was meddling dangerously with their lives was brought out into the light.

When she finished with the new saloon's business, she turned her chair to face him and watched him sleep. Another hour passed with her gazing at him, feeling quite content, although she would choke anyone who ever found out. She wasn't yearning exactly, just studying him. There was something so restful and alluring about the relaxed lines of his face, the way his eyelashes fanned his proud cheekbones. *What a looker, he was!*

At that moment, Carter stirred. When he opened his eyes, he gazed directly into hers. He grinned.

"What is it?" she asked, wondering what could bring on that sensual smile so quickly.

"I can't remember ever waking up to a more welcome view in my life."

She shook her head. "You are a sweet talker."

His face turned serious. "No, Jo, I mean it." In the next second, he held open his arms, beckoning her.

She caught her breath, hesitating. She knew what he was offering. At least, she thought she did. And if she accepted his offer, there was no going back, at least for her.

Almost involuntarily, she stood up and took a step toward him. Then another. *Is this what I want?* she asked herself. *Or did she want more than he could give her?*

He took hold of her hands and pulled her down on top of him. There she was, sprawled across Jameson Carter—at last!—reveling in the bay rum scent of him and the warmth of his body.

His hand found its way into her hair, cupping the back of her head, drawing her down. A last glance into his eyes before she closed hers confirmed a blaze of desire as keen as her own. She let him bring her the last few inches until their lips met.

And she melted. Every bone in her body became jelly, and her limbs were inexplicably languid. His tongue explored her mouth, slowly and thoroughly, until she sucked on it, halting its progress. She heard him groan, and something deep inside her shifted.

He lowered both his hands to grasp her buttocks and pull her tightly against his hard maleness. She gasped, startled by the potency of the craving coursing through her. It had been so ridiculously long since...

"Jo," he murmured against her lips.

"Mm." She couldn't even speak. Didn't want to. The world was tilting.

No, she was. Carter had rolled over until she lay firmly on her back, looking up at his devastatingly handsome yet dear face.

He rose up, his hands on either side of her.

"I want you so much," he confessed, making a glow of happiness ignite inside her.

Forever? She banished the wishful thought and nodded, which he took quite rightly as her agreement.

He reared back so he could begin unbuttoning his shirt, while she watched with interest. It hit the floor in a few seconds. Then he started to unbutton her blouse, which she allowed until it was open to her waistband, exposing her corset and low-cut shift.

"We've got too many clothes on to undress properly lying down," she pointed out.

"True," he agreed. "It will take us all day at this rate."

He was right, and she for one felt too eager to take all day.

"Let me up," she ordered, and they both stood. When she removed her blouse, he watched her, while at the same time kicking off his shoes. Then he unbuckled his belt, making her mouth go dry. Finally, he dropped his pants to the floor, standing in his cotton unmentionables.

When at last she'd unfastened her corset, she was left in only her lacey, thigh-length shift, her stockings, and a smile.

"Lord have mercy," he muttered, and she felt her smile lift her cheeks.

"You affect me the same way, Carter."

"Why don't you call me Jameson?"

"Why don't you kiss me again?"

"Remove your holster," he ordered, gesturing to her ankle where her derringer glinted wickedly. "And I'll do precisely that."

"Fair enough," she said, surprised at how her voice sounded like a soft purr. She undid the strap and placed it beside her shoes.

He bent down and unhooked her stockings from her garter belt, which he removed with a quick flick. Slowly, he rolled her sheer white stockings down her legs, leaving a trail of goose flesh where his fingers touched her. She shivered.

He rose to his feet and pulled her close before kissing her as promised, a long fiery fusing of their mouths that left them both panting for more. When he brushed his knuckles across her still-shielded nipples, she arched against him. Hurriedly, he slipped the sheer shift off her shoulders and let it fall, revealing all her generous curves.

"Your body has teased and tormented me for a very long time," he acknowledged.

In a heartbeat—a thudding, throbbing, chest-aching beat—she found herself on her back again on the soft hotel bed.

"I've wanted you stark naked and lying under me for what feels like a hundred years."

Feeling giddy with desire and delight, she laughed lightly at his words, aware her breasts bounced, drawing his fascinated gaze. He lowered his head and brushed his lips against one dusky nipple then the other.

"*Mm,*" she murmured, and let him feast on her for a few minutes.

"When we do this," he said, "you're mine. I don't share."

That sobered her. She didn't know whether to take offense he thought her so loose a woman he had to explain his philosophy, or to be flattered by his possessive tone.

"Likewise," she retorted. Exclusivity suited her just fine, especially where Carter was concerned. She might have lain before with a man for the sheer enjoyment of it, but she'd never done so when she was promised to another.

Nor did she want a man who belonged to another woman.

Without further preamble, he sunk into her slick warmth and filled her, making her suck in her breath.

"Too fast?" he whispered against her neck.

"Just fine," she replied. She rocked her hips, and he thrust again, repeating the rapture and sending her into immediate bliss.

"I knew it would feel like this with you," he said against her skin. Then his mouth left that sensitive place on her neck, as he lifted his head and gazed into her eyes.

"Me, too," she said, her voice a throaty whisper.

He pulled back and then slowly filled her again. She couldn't help the moan of pure pleasure, astonished to find herself already close to the edge. Trembling, her insides fluttering, she was hot all over and throbbing.

Leaning on his forearms, he paused long enough to claim her mouth again under his, kissing her with tiny nibbling kisses, alternately sucking on her lower lip as he continued to stroke deep inside her. His tongue slipped into her welcoming mouth to mimic the thrusting of his body.

She groaned, sucking on his tongue until he groaned, too.

In another moment, she felt his mouth trace a fiery trail, caressing her throat as far down as he could reach while still staying firmly sheathed in her snug passage.

She arched again, beginning to shudder in response to the tightening at the core of her body.

"Beautiful," he murmured.

She shattered under him, the rolling waves of pleasure so great and her release so long and powerful, it left her utterly sapped. His body quivered and then held still, having plunged as far inside her as he could, holding there, motionless. A second later, he pulled out quickly and spent himself beside her.

He didn't collapse on top of her as she expected, but rather, rolled to the side so they were face-to-face, their heads on the pillow, legs still entwined.

"Have mercy!" He regarded her with a look that was nothing short of stunned.

She imagined she wore a similar expression. *What should she say, if anything?*

"Do you think we should get out of here before someone sets fire to the hotel?" she quipped.

Whoops, wrong thing apparently. It was meant to be a little jest, but it only served to banish his dreamy look and replace it with a solemn one. He ran a finger along her cheekbone.

"I think you ought to move immediately into my cabin on the boat, so we can look out for one another."

Her heart gave a flutter. Being of practical nature, she liked the image of a common cause of self-preservation. She would have hated if he'd declared he had to do all the protecting. Instead, he'd stated it as a mutual partnership.

Regardless, no matter how tempting Carter's offer, she was used to taking care of herself, and she intended to continue doing so.

"We might go down with the ship together," she pointed out, making light of his suggestion. "Your vessel hasn't proven to be the safest place either."

"Darla," he recalled with a wince. "I should get back and see how she's faring."

Jo nodded but noticed he wasn't hurrying from her bed. He was still tracing her jaw and then brushing his thumb across her lips.

"Will you come with me?" he asked again.

She kissed him once more. When they finally pulled apart for air, he added, "I don't think I could stand to have you out of my sight. And if anything happened to you now, when I've finally got you right where I want you...," he trailed off and shot her a weak smile, clearly worried.

Dodging his question, she asked, "Who would want us both dead?"

That seemed to be the objective, even if, so far, the would-be killer had failed.

"The only connection we have to violence is that man from your saloon."

"Frank Hirsch?" She pondered the man's name for a moment. "And we know *he's* not aiming at us."

"Maybe an angry wife?" Jameson pondered, stroking her shoulder.

"Nope." Jo was hardly able to believe she was having this conversation while naked in bed with Carter. "Frank didn't have any family, at least not in Keokuk or in Hamilton, not that I'm aware of."

"That you're aware of."

"Well, I do get around," she reminded him. Realizing the implication of her words, she averted her gaze, pained to imagine what he thought of her and her occupation.

But he turned her face back to his with a firm hold.

"It's all right. I knew what you meant. You hear everything in your position. I hear quite a bit, too, although I think when men are at The Pork, they're more openly communicative than when gambling at my place."

And just as before, a shot rang out, sounding as if it were directly outside her hotel window in the street below. Jo rolled her eyes, more annoyed than scared.

"We've got to take care of this," she said, sitting up. "It has to stop."

"Agreed," Carter said, at the same time pulling her back down and over the edge of the bed with him. "But you can't do anything with a bullet in your head."

He scrambled around gathering his clothing, and she did the same. As she wriggled into her skirt, anger bloomed within her, growing from a simmer to a rolling boil.

Yes, she was mighty pissed off. First her saloon, then Carter's boat.

It was no surprise when a woman started shrieking outside the front of the hotel, making the skin on Jo's nape prickle. *Now, what?*

CHAPTER TEN

Jameson's hand tightened around Jo's, slowing her pell-mell rush down the hotel stairs to the exit. The scene they had just witnessed from their window flashed before his eyes—Jo's trim, black gelding lying maimed in the street, a gaping hole in its side, blood widening in a pool around it.

The gruesome sight awaiting them made him pull her to a halt on the landing.

"Jo, wait. It could be a trap."

"Or just a threat," she countered, amazing him that she could keep her wits at such a moment. The sheen of tears brightening her wide eyes was the only indication the horror awaiting them outside had upset her.

Jameson had not seen Jo come unhinged before. Apparently, from what he'd heard, she'd escaped the fire with cool aplomb, and he'd seen for himself how well she'd handled being shot at. Now, faced with seeing her horse, a bullet in its side, lying wild-eyed and bleeding from its mouth, his heart broke for her. Whoever did this was one mean son of a bitch!

He pulled her into a brief embrace before tugging her to follow behind him as he led her cautiously through the exit.

They went through unnoticed, the door left ajar by the many people pouring outside to witness the atrocity, joining those already in the street.

"Step aside, please. Let us through," he ordered, feeling safe enough in the presence of so many to expose them to whoever had shot the horse.

As they came upon the fallen animal, Jo sank to her knees, bending over to stroke her horse's muzzle and murmur reassurances while she looked it over at the same time, apparently noting the severity of its injury. However, when she held out her hand to him, Jameson didn't know what she wanted.

When he didn't respond immediately, she leaped up and snatched his revolver out of its holster. Pausing for a moment to gather her resolve, he watched her swallow hard, lift the gun with a slightly trembling hand, and shoot the gelding between the eyes. Jameson jumped even though he saw it coming. The horse went immediately limp, released from its agony.

Then Jo stood back, whipping her hair over one shoulder, looked to the heavens, and screamed. Not a feminine shriek of terror either. No, she let out a primal yell of anger that silenced everyone around them. He almost felt sorry for whoever had done this. She was going to make someone pay with his hide, no mercy given.

With a stiff spine and without looking at him, Jo handed him back his revolver. With its bullet so much larger than her derringer, she'd known it was certain to kill the horse in one shot, and it had done the job.

Turning away, she walked silently back into the hotel lobby.

Jameson paid a man to cart the horse away and then hurried to follow her. He expected to find her crying in the privacy of her room. Instead, she stood at her window, staring down at the scene of the carcass being removed.

Not turning around when he entered, she said, "I want to personally slay this bastard with my bare hands."

"I'm sorry, Jo."

She lifted a hand and waved away his condolence. "Just a horse," she muttered, although he heard a catch in her voice. "But a damn fine one who didn't deserve this."

"I know," he said, and put a hand on her slender shoulder. Not an hour ago, he'd had his mouth on it, kissing her silky skin.

She flinched slightly but let him turn her to face him. Her features were pinched, and he wished there was something he could do to take away her pain and anger.

"What was its name?" he asked.

As if she hadn't expected such a sentimental question, her eyes widened, glistening as the tears he'd been expecting made their first appearance.

"Daisy," she whispered. Sure enough, first one salty drop then another slipped down her lovely cheeks. She dashed them aside with her knuckle before he could, and he watched her pull herself together.

He paused, frowning with puzzlement. "But it was a gelding."

She sighed. "I know. I just liked the name."

Amused by her unexpected whimsy of giving a castrated male horse the sweet name of Daisy, he brushed his lips across her forehead, and then he simply held her. He would have been content to stand that way all the rest of his life, with his hands on her back, holding her close. Eventually, she took a deep breath and pushed at him.

"You have to go," she reminded him. "Check on Darla."

"I know," he agreed.

"Send word to me how she's doing." Jo's voice was steady again, and he felt his admiration for her swell.

"Why don't you come back with me?" he asked, hearkening back to his earlier offer, despite already knowing her answer.

Turning slightly, she averted her face.

"No, I'm not moving to your boat. That's not who I am, Carter, someone who hands her problems over to someone else, namely you. Nor do I hide from trouble."

"This isn't only your problem. I think it's *ours*."

"We don't know for certain. Anyway, I'll be all right. There are a lot of people around, and I have my gun."

"And I know you'll use it," he said, reaching up to tuck her hair behind her ear. Then the question uppermost in his mind slipped out of him. "Miss Holland, would you consider being my gal?"

Her mouth formed a delightful "O." Apparently, he'd succeeded in astonishing her. And thankfully, she wasn't frowning or turning him down outright.

"You can't truly be surprised," he added.

But clearly, she was. She put her hands up to her cheeks before clasping them in front of her.

"Female saloon owners, especially madams, don't get asked that question very often. At least, this one hasn't."

"Do I get an answer?" he asked.

She angled her chin into the air. "I suppose I need to know what being your gal entails."

Her practical reply tickled a chuckle out of him.

"Whatever you want, Jo. Whatever you're ready for. I'm fairly easy on the particulars. As long as it's just you and me, then I'll be fine with the arrangement."

She cocked her head, looking him up and down as if he were a rack of ribs at the butcher's shop.

"In that case, I suppose I can't say no. We'll sew together the details next time we meet."

"Which will be when?" he prompted, still reluctant to leave her behind.

"Are you going to demand all my time?" she teased.

He slipped his arms around her waist again. "As much as you'll give me."

Holding her close felt like the most natural thing in the world, just as waking up and seeing her had instantly seemed right. He didn't think it would be too much longer before he'd be offering her his hand and his name.

Lowering his head, he touched his lips to hers, feeling her melt against him. She was all luscious and warm, curves and softness, and he had to remind himself he was heading out the door.

"You were just leaving," she said, reading his mind.

"I know. I want to see you later. I'll come back, or do you want to come to the boat?"

She hesitated.

"I know you're not too busy," he prompted. "No saloon to run at the moment."

"Unfortunately, that's true. However, I don't want you to get too used to my company."

"Why not? Let's get used to it," he insisted. "I think we could both use the companionship."

He kissed her again, feeling her hands against his chest, grabbing onto his shirt.

"Go," she said, "I'll see you later. If I'm not at your boat by, say, seven o'clock, you can come here and we'll have dinner."

He grinned. "Deal."

To get to Pete's house, Jo had to hire a taxi now that Daisy was gone. She would replace her horse, but not today. A suspicion this was all connected to Frank Hirsch had her worrying over Pete and his little family. As far as she knew, he didn't carry a gun, but only kept the shotgun behind the bar. He was a brawny man, and no one normally picked a fight with her partner. But whoever would shoot a horse out of spite was not normal.

She was relieved to see Emily hanging washing in the side yard in the full afternoon sun. Pete sat on the porch and had his little one with him, watching him play while tapping his hand on the armrest of his chair.

"You look at loose ends, too," Jo said by way of greeting. "I heard you checked on the workmen today already."

"You know it. I'll do so every day, twice a day. They don't want to see me again, but they're working lickety-split."

"You're doing something right," she said, with admiration. "I was just over there, and I've never seen a building transforming so quickly."

He nodded toward the taxi she had waiting at his gate. "What's with that?"

She told him briefly, leaving out how she'd had to administer the *coup de grâce. Poor Daisy.*

A scowl gathered on his forehead as she spun her tale.

"That's strange and unsettling, Miss Josephine, and I'm sorry for the loss of good horseflesh, quick and smart as it was, too. But send the taxi away. I'll take you back later. Stay for supper."

Two thoughts popped into her brain. One, she didn't want Pete leaving his family unprotected. She would never forgive herself if he was out driving her and someone came gunning for him, hitting his wife or son instead. And two, she'd decided to go to Carter's boat after all, and this time behave herself and not get tossed off. She intended to stay only for the one night, however, and only to explore further where their new arrangement might lead.

But she didn't particularly want her business partner knowing where she was going to spend her evening, either.

Reassured all was fine with Pete, Jo turned down his offer and returned to her hotel. When she'd stalled all she could by browsing the Keokuk shops, buying some new undergarments, and purchasing a copy of *Madam Bovary* to see what kind of madam she was, Jo took a taxi to Carter's boat.

With it bustling as usual, she easily boarded unnoticed. It was a very different scenario than when her friend Thaddeus had asked her to distract the entire boatload of gamblers so he could rescue the love of his life.

At that time, Jo had made sure every man-jack had seen her grand entrance and kept his eyes on her. She didn't know if Carter had witnessed her display, or merely heard about it. *If he was there, had he been entirely distracted by her, too?*

Jo stopped at the bar in the lower-level gaming room and ordered a glass of wine. Lucille, she noticed, stood next to a flush-faced man with a stack of chips in front of him, who kept reaching out a hand to squeeze her rear end. Or try to. Lucille dodged successfully while holding her ground, clearly determined to make a go of a position to which she was entirely ill-suited.

Jo pursed her lips. Her girls were used to better clientele and rarely let themselves be groped. *Her girls!* God, how she missed them and her business. But that was before the fire and stolen it away and before bullets started flying in her direction.

At that moment, as if on cue, she felt a hand on her shoulder, and she nearly shrieked aloud.

CHAPTER ELEVEN

Candace was beside her, a huge smile gracing her gorgeous face.

"Oh, Miss Josephine, it is so good to see you." The girl stepped right into Jo's open arms for a hug.

"How are you doing, honey? Are they treating you well?" Jo asked, now that her ridiculously jumpy nerves had settled.

Candace looked around the crowded room. "It's different. The pay isn't so good and the hours are longer."

"You look mighty fine in that gown," Jo offered. "Class and sass!"

"True," Candace agreed, sliding her hands down and over her generous hips.

"Ah, here's my lovely dance partner," said a handsome man in his prime coming up behind her. "I have a dollar here that's begging to be yours."

"That's the silliest thing I've ever heard," Candace remarked. "A begging dollar!" But she winked at Jo before letting the man lead her away through the crowd, no doubt to find a place on deck where they could sway under the stars.

Satisfied her girl was happy, Jo made her way up to the deck on the next level and looked for Carter. No sign of him. Ben was there watching over things, and he spotted her almost immediately.

"Oh, lordy," she muttered as he made a line for her as straight as the crow flew.

"Welcome, Miss Holland," Ben said, not looking the least bit welcoming.

"Don't get your knickers in a twist," she said, flashing him the smile that had made a man bestow a ruby on her once. "I'm not here to cause trouble. I was invited."

"You were invited last time I believe, which didn't deter you from assaulting our newest hire."

So much for a winning smile. She decided to change tactics. "How is Miss Darla?"

Ben relaxed a little. "She'll survive unless infection sets in. Mr. Carter feels terrible she took a bullet meant for him."

"I know he does," Jo said. "And the boat?"

"Sound as a gold dollar now. It was minimal damage. Had it repaired this afternoon."

His stance had eased, the initial tension gone. Jo knew she was asking all the right questions.

"That's good. Where is Carter anyhow?"

"Top deck, I think. You want me to tell him you're here?"

"No, thank you," Jo said, relieved he had made the offer instead of wanting to escort her off the boat. "Don't let me interrupt whatever you were doing. I'll be good, I promise," she added with a backward glance.

This time, Ben gave her a wry smile in return, and she knew she'd won him over. If she was going to be Carter's girl, she'd better get along with his right-hand man, who was clearly also his friend.

Carter was talking with two other men but excused himself the moment his eyes lit on her when she crested the stairs.

"There's my lady," he said as she approached.

Jo took a sip of her wine to hide her pleasure. *This was too "normal," wasn't it?* But she couldn't back down now. Her heart was in too deep.

"Ben said Darla is holding her own," she said by way of greeting.

He nodded, looking a bit weary still.

"I guess you're like family here," Jo observed, "the way Pete and I are with our girls."

"Precisely. So you came," Carter added, stating the obvious.

She sought to make light of it. "I thought I'd save you another trip across the river today."

He moved a step closer. "I would cross the river fifty times a day to see you," he vowed, his eyes burning with intensity. Lifting her wine glass from her, he took a long drink without asking.

"But I appreciate you did so because it's been a hellish couple of days," he said. "Will you stay tonight?"

She was mesmerized for a moment by the intimate act of him drinking from her glass, imagining his lips elsewhere. *Would she stay?* She tilted her head and seemed to consider despite having already made a decision.

"Seeing as I don't have a ride back."

His smile spread slowly, and he returned her glass to her deliberately brushing her fingers with his.

"What time will you close up tonight?" she asked.

"Whenever you want me to."

That made her laugh. "That's no way to run a business, Carter."

"I'd shut the whole damn boat down now and toss everyone into the river if you asked me to."

Her eyes widened. "I must have been very good this morning."

He paused and drew his eyebrows together.

"This isn't only about that, and you know it." Then his expression lightened. "But yes, you were very good this morning."

After that, she left him alone to chat with his customers, solve a dispute at one of the gaming tables below, and get the ladies singing when a diversion was needed. She didn't catch sight of Lucille again or have to hear her warbling. She was impressed by how adept Carter was at handling every situation although not at all surprised.

Meanwhile, she played and won a few games of monte, and ordered a meal that was on the house when she tried to pay. Apparently, Carter had already told each of his employees where she and he stood.

What an amazing man—confessing to his staff that his new lady friend was a saloon owner and a madam. She'd never expected such a boon. He couldn't possibly know how during her infrequent returns to Chicago, some snooty folks had cut her every which way, directly, indirectly, and sublimely. People crossed the street, tied their shoes, and even gazed at the clouds to avoid greeting her. Yet she had a feeling Carter wouldn't give a tinker's curse what others thought, and she smiled at her good fortune.

Hours later, an irritating voice sounded in her ear.

"I can't believe you're here again," Lucille exclaimed on a note that set Jo's teeth on edge. "Have you no shame?"

The temptation to toss the girl to the ground for the second time rose up swiftly in Jo. Recalling she'd promised Ben she wouldn't cause any trouble, however, she satisfied herself by leveling the biddy with a stare.

"Is there a reason you're speaking to me? I don't want to dance with you, nor do I care for your singing. Don't approach me again unless I call you over to get me a drink."

Lucille glared. "I'd as likely toss it in your face."

Jo raised an eyebrow. "I hope you do. That will be the end of your employment on this boat, and I won't have to lift a finger to get rid of you."

Lucille stamped her foot. "You'll be sorry. In fact, you already are. You just don't know it yet." And she turned and walked away.

Sorry? Doubtful. *Goaded into doing bodily harm?* More likely.

But Jo released her thoughts of Lucille like a fisherman releases a walleye when hunting for catfish. The rest of her evening passed with growing anticipation. Finally, she heard Ben give the last call, much the way Pete would in their saloon. It wasn't long after that she watched the late-night gamblers leave, with Ben and Carter escorting any stragglers off the boat.

Ben left next for his house in Hamilton, a wife and two daughters waiting at home, as he told Jo.

At last, she watched Carter approach her where she sat on a stool by the bar, chatting with the bartender.

"Having a good time?" Carter asked her, his eyes sparkling when he looked her over.

Jo could swear her skin tingled wherever his gaze touched. "I am."

He crossed his arms. "Usually, I'm rather weary by this time, but not tonight. Right now, I'm feeling a burst of vigor."

"Does that mean you're not ready to turn in?" Jo asked, widening her eyes and wondering if she managed to look at all innocent.

Apparently not. Carter's eyes crinkled with wicked amusement.

"Harry, pour me a double brandy and go home," he said to his bartender without taking his eyes off of her. He waited for his drink to be slid across the counter to him, and then he took her hand.

"Now I'm ready."

Jo's heartbeat was galloping like a wild pony on the plains. Feeling a sense of déjà vu, she accompanied Carter to the captain's stateroom. Quite a different set of circumstances than the last time she'd been there.

Jo bit her lip. She'd never explained herself to anyone in her life. Yet as she entered the cabin, she felt the overwhelming need to make sure Carter knew they were not going over old ground.

Placing her reticule on his bureau, she unbuttoned her short, fitted silk jacket, which she laid on a chair. Carter leaned against the door watching her, arms crossed, brandy in hand. She knew what was on his mind, the past—her past, to be precise.

"Just so you know, and I'll only say this once and be done, your old boss was unable to make a full salute. He had a 'lazy lob,' if you understand what I'm saying."

"Oh," Carter said and nothing more. His narrowed eyes told her nothing. Perhaps he was imagining what else she might have done with his old boss.

"I gave Stoddard merely a show, and it was all I ever intended to give him." She hoped to obliterate any doubts Carter might still have about aligning himself romantically with what many perceived her to be, a glorified harlot.

His jaw tightened as he most likely envisioned what that meant, and she wondered if even that was too much for him to accept. *Was he already regretting his offer to have her as his lady friend?*

However, after a moment, he nodded and sipped his drink, then handed the glass to her.

"Will you give me a show right now?" he asked, on a hopeful note.

As her uncertainty eased, she released the breath she'd been holding and took a sip of the fine brandy. And all at once, she was sure he would never let her go.

"I will," she promised, setting the glass aside. "And a lot more."

Jo removed the rest of her clothing under his appreciative gaze. She'd been extra careful choosing her underthings, wearing all satin and lace—red, of course—which she'd purchased earlier in the day. Carter's flared nostrils and darkening gaze told her she'd chosen well.

When she stood before him in the skimpiest of satin underthings, he hauled her into his arms faster than a duck diving on a June bug.

"You are exquisite," he told her. "Why haven't you been scooped up by some man and spirited away?"

She snaked her arms up and around his neck, relishing the sensation of her breasts squeezing out of her half corset and pressing against his vest and shirt.

"A few have tried, but they didn't capture my interest. Why haven't you been tied to some pretty lady's apron strings?"

He nuzzled her neck, and his lips on her skin felt like paradise, if paradise was a searing brand.

"I'm not the apron string–type, I guess. I prefer my women independent and with a little zest."

"And *I* have zest?" she asked, as he lowered a hand to cup her lace-clad bottom and tilt her into him.

"You have it in spades, Jo."

His other hand stroked along her collar bone and then dipped below the top of her corset to brush against her nipples, one, then the other.

"My legs are going to buckle in about ten seconds," she confessed. "Can we move this to your bed?"

In answer, he lifted her in his arms and laid her down gently on his coverlet. He had just bent his head to kiss the swell of her breast when knuckles made contact with his door.

"Christ!" he exclaimed. "What on God's green earth?" Then more loudly, he asked, "Who is it?"

"It's Lucille."

It was Jo's turn to swear, but Carter put a hand to her lips.

"This isn't a good time, Miss Strong," he called out.

"There's a woman here named Emily Carlisle," Lucille persisted. "She says her husband has been injured."

Jo gasped at the unexpected statement. "That's Pete's wife," she exclaimed, pushing at Carter's chest so she could sit. He rolled off the bed, and she jumped up, getting dressed as quickly as she'd undressed. Before she was done, however, Carter had slipped out of the room.

When Jo found him in the gaming room, he was with Emily, who was crying and holding their little one.

"Oh, Miss Josephine," she bawled when she saw her. "Pete's been hurt bad."

"How?" She was terrified she would hear he'd been shot. An image of the blood pouring out of Daisy brought the bile into her throat.

"Strangest thing," Emily said. "He went round the side of the house and stepped in a coyote trap."

Jo closed her eyes for a second, as if she could shut out the news of Pete's injury.

"How bad?" she heard Carter ask.

"Bad enough. Nothing gets to my Pete, but he was hollerin' something to wake the dead. It took both me and my pa to get the trap off of him. But if it had been our little boy who'd stepped in it…" She hugged the child to her and started to cry again.

"Where is Pete now?" Jo asked.

"At home with the doctor. Pete told me to come tell you, either one of you."

Jo shot Carter a look. "There's no doubt now this has to be related."

"I agree." His expression matched her grim disposition.

"Come on, Emily," Jo said. "I'll take you ho . . . Oh for God's sake, I don't have my carriage or a horse."

"I'll take her," Carter said, "and I'll check on Pete. I think it's better if I go in case there's more danger. Maybe I should hire someone to watch their house. Mrs. Carlisle, can your father stay with you to keep an eye out in case there's trouble?"

Emily frowned. "What's he talking about, Miss Josephine? What kind of trouble?"

"Answer him, honey," Jo prompted. "Is your father fit enough, and can he use a gun?"

"Yes," Emily said, her voice barely above a whisper.

"On the other hand, maybe I should bring them all back here," Carter suggested to Jo.

She loved that he offered, even though there was not enough room unless they started sleeping in the gaming rooms.

Emily shook her head. "The doctor said he can't be moved. Not immediately anyway. I'd like to get back to him now. You two have me afeared all over again."

"It'll be all right, Mrs. Carlisle," Carter told her, and Jo prayed to Heaven he was right.

"Just make sure things are settled," Jo seconded, holding his gaze. "I think a hired man is a good idea."

CHAPTER TWELVE

Leaning on the railing in the darkness, illuminated only by the lamps Ben had lit earlier on the dock, Jo watched them depart. She kept watching until she couldn't see them anymore. After that, regret coursed through her, realizing she would spend every moment worrying until Carter returned. She should have insisted she go with him.

Lord but she was exhausted! She rested her chin on her hands and her elbows on the railing. Carter must be even worse. He was into his second night with little sleep except for the catnap in her hotel room that morning. *That morning!* Her mind ranged over their delicious encounter. The way he'd looked at her, touched her, whispered in her ear. Every part of her body set to prickling just thinking about him. And his laugh. And his eyes. And his sensual, firm lips.

How she loved this man! Lifting her head, she slapped a hand over her mouth as if she'd spoken out loud. Then she groaned into the darkness. God, she was head over heels in love with Jameson Carter.

She tapped on the railing, feeling antsy. *What could she do to keep busy until he returned?* Just then, one of the dock lights snuffed out with a strange little popping explosion.

What the hell? Exhausted as her body felt, nervous energy zapped through her limbs. She waited, her gaze traveling from the dim dock to the now pitch-black stern of the boat, listening intently. However, there was nothing to see and nothing to hear.

And then another lamp went out. She could swear all the hair on her head stood up.

"Who's out there?" she called out.

Silence.

Footsteps behind her had Jo whirling where she stood, jumpy as a cat next to a rocking chair. Candace stood there, pulling a wrap around her.

"You startled me," Jo admitted. "Why are you up?"

"I still find it a little strange, sleeping on a boat. It's not natural. I was awake and went for a glass of wine." The young woman held it up as evidence. "Mr. Carter said he didn't mind if we helped ourselves to some now and then. When it got dark out here all of a sudden. I thought maybe a storm was coming."

Jo glanced back at the dark dock. "No, just some faulty lamps, I guess."

Candace nodded. "Things happen on the river."

That didn't help to calm Jo's nerves. And when Candace bid her goodnight, she nearly asked the girl to stay up with her, but didn't.

Pull yourself together, Jo scolded herself and wandered back into the gaming room, deciding a glass of good brandy from Carter's stock would soothe her and help make the interminable vigil more tolerable.

After all, it was just her and his ladies, even if it was black as Hades outside. Jo had her derringer, and unless someone tossed a stick of dynamite blowing them out of the water, she was determined to defend the riverboat in Carter's absence.

Jameson winced at the deep gashes on Pete Carlisle's leg. The man was lucky he hadn't lost his foot altogether. Fortunately, he wore tough buffalo hide boots, which took a some of the impact and probably saved him from losing his leg altogether.

Emily fussed over her husband and their young son fussed beside her. Jameson grabbed her pa for a private word outside.

"You need to be armed and remain vigilant. This wasn't an accident."

"I figured that," the man spat out. "No one puts a trap like that at the bottom of the steps unless they're off their chump or nail-spittin' angry at someone."

"Both perhaps," Jameson agreed. "You have a gun?"

"Yup, and I'll shoot the first man who comes to threaten my Emily or her family."

"I think the target will be Pete again."

The older man nodded. Jameson went back inside to talk to Pete.

"You have to protect Miss Josephine," were the first words out of the bartender's mouth.

Jameson nodded. "I'm going to insist she stay on the boat with me. The Fairview is too open. She'd be vulnerable to anyone going in and straight upstairs to her room. She thinks she can protect herself with—"

"With that little toy gun of hers," Pete cut in, then grimaced as he shifted himself. "I feel like a damn fool. Or a hog-tied calf. I can barely move."

"We've all been targets," Jameson said. "I'd better get back. Your father-in-law will watch over your house. And we'll figure this out before anyone else gets hurt." He hoped.

The unease that had grown since he'd left his boat—and left Jo behind—blossomed into full agitation, making his scalp tighten. He fairly ran to his horse and kept it at a full gallop across the bridge and all the way home. It didn't help his anxiety when he approached his dock and saw that there were no lamps lit, and he always had at least on the leeward sign and one on the other.

Perhaps Jo had put them out, worried about fire. Perhaps there'd been a malfunction, and Jo hadn't noticed but had fallen asleep. That wouldn't be a surprise. At this point, Jameson knew he could just about sleep standing up.

Not a sound emanated from his boat as he crossed the dock. Even the river was still, causing barely a whisper of a ripple against the hull as he stepped onboard. His own footfalls sounded loud and heavy in the silence, and an unexpected frisson of fear skated up his backbone.

He'd been certain Jo would wait up to hear word of Pete's condition. The other ladies, of course, would be in their beds.

Upon entering the lower-level gaming room, he climbed the inner staircase to the luxurious upper-level chamber. At the sound of his footsteps, a lamp flared to life, and for a split second, he started to smile, imagining Jo was waiting for him in the darkness in her sinfully red satin.

However, the scene that emerged was not a sensual dream but a nightmare. Jo sat at a table on which the lamp had just been lit next to an empty brandy glass. Lucille Strong, standing on the other side of the table, tossed an extinguished match into the glass. She had a pistol trained on Jo.

"Ah, the viper has returned to his nest," Lucille intoned, slowly directing her gun toward him.

"What the hell's going on?" Jameson asked. *Had the ladies gotten into another fight with Jo on the losing end this time?* Instinctively, he knew there was more to it.

Then he noticed Jo's mouth was bound with a cloth tied behind her head. Her hands, however, were on the table in plain sight. Most likely, Lucille hadn't wanted to get close enough to tie her up in case Jo overpowered her in the process.

"Sit down," Lucille ordered. Then she sighed. "Mr. Carlisle isn't with you? I was hoping you'd bring him back here to make it easier for me. But I'll get him tomorrow." She angled her head and looked at his holster. "I think I'll use *your* gun to kill *her* partner. Nice touch, don't you think?"

"Why are you doing this?" Jameson asked, not taking a step closer to the table. Once he sat as she wanted, he would literally be a sitting duck. And he had no intention of going down easy.

"Simple. An eye for an eye. You gunned down my brother in cold blood." She cocked the trigger. "I told you to sit down."

He took a single deliberate step forward. Jo had been wrong about Frank not having any family. He risked taking his eyes off the flushed and livid face of Lucille, and looked at Jo. She struck him as more angry than frightened. Her eyes were glaring at Frank's sister, then narrowing when she looked at him, in warning perhaps.

"Can she remove her gag?" he asked, hoping to get a little more help if Jo was able to talk.

"It was a pleasure finally shutting her up," Lucille said. "And doing it permanently will be even better."

She *was* insane, he thought.

"But if you take a seat and put your gun on the table," Lucille added, "I'll let her take it off. One wrong move and I'll put a bullet in her heart right quick."

"Understood," he said. He risked another glance at Jo. Her spiritedness worried him in this situation. "You behave, too," he told her. "No heroics."

His feisty lady rolled her eyes in response.

Lucille watched Jameson take a seat and slowly draw out his gun before laying it on the table.

"You can take the gag off," she said to Jo, not taking her eyes off Jameson.

Jo did so, untying the cloth—one of the cook's bandanas—and yanking it off.

"That was disgusting," she declared, wiping her mouth.

Jameson noticed she returned only one of her hands to the tabletop. The other disappeared into her lap.

"Shut up," Lucille said sharply. "*You* are disgusting! Luring my brother, a God-serving preacher, into your foul establishment and then . . . then," she faltered and her voice caught. "You murdered him, like Jezebel slaughtering the prophets."

Jo's gaze shot to Jameson.

"So, you're Frank's sister?" he asked, thinking to calm her down with a little chitchat and draw her attention away from Jo.

"Shut up," Lucille said again. "Don't you dare say his name, unless you do so with respect."

"All right," Jameson tried again. "Did Reverend. Hirsch have any other family?" *Other lunatics who are going to come gunning for us if you fail?*

"Just me. You took the only kin I had left in this world and sent him home in an eternity box. And all for what, a toss on the sheets with this one?" She jerked her head toward Jo.

Jameson figured Jo wasn't correcting Lucille in order to protect her ladies, particularly Madeleine. No need to endanger the real object of Frank's lust and the true cause of his going berserk with frustration.

"He'd been serving the Lord for so long," Lucille continued, "he probably wanted to help this strumpet to see the errors of her ways, to help her escape the fires of hell. I tried to send her to eternal damnation by fire. Now, I'm going to send you both there for what you did. So, who wants to lay down the knife and fork first?" Lucille asked suddenly, swinging her gun from one to the other.

CHAPTER THIRTEEN

Jo fumed. First, she found the euphemism for death to be
particularly vulgar. The only place she wanted to put a knife or
a fork was into Lucille's heart. Secondly, this mad woman had
caught her off-guard and by surprise, drawing a gun on her while
she sat and waited for Carter. She'd been unable to talk her way
out of the ambush, and now Carter was in the thick of trouble
with her.

"How will you live with yourself after hurting innocent
people?" she asked Frank's sister.

"I won't hurt any innocent people," Lucille protested,

"You already have," Jo insisted. "All my girls lost their home
and are out of work."

Lucille merely shrugged, waving her pistol in the air to
dismiss the statement.

"Saloon whores are not innocent people!"

"What about my horse?" Jo asked, thinking of her sweet
Daisy.

Lucille looked at her as if she were a simpleton.

"An animal! We're talking about my brother. Shot down in cold blood in your disgusting brothel, lured there by your drink and easy women, and by you."

Jo decided that bad-mouthing Frank by telling Lucille the truth of how often he visited was not going to help. Most likely, she'd get herself shot faster.

Instead, she asked, "And what about my bartender? Why did you set the trap for him?"

However, before Lucille could answer her, Jo turned to Carter.

"How is Pete?"

And as easy as that, while Lucille became distracted by their conversation, Jo started to slide her hand from her lap down her leg toward her holster. She saw Carter's eyes widen nearly imperceptibly as he tracked her movements.

"Pete's hurting," he told her, "but nothing fatal. He'll have a limp for sure."

"No, he won't," Lucille interrupted, "because I intend to kill him shortly. The trap was just to slow him down so I'd know where he was after I finished with you two. And if you'd brought him here, then like the angel of the Lord, I would've got you all at once, the way you all murdered Frank."

"Thou shalt not kill," Jo reminded her, figuring nothing would make an impression on the preacher's sister except biblical words. However, Lucille turned a cold stare upon her.

"Behave as a barbarian," she said, "and you'll be treated like one."

"You call Miss Holland a barbarian when you set a steel coyote trap on a man," Carter scoffed, and Jo sent him a silent thanks for taking Lucille's attention once more.

"That terrible man!" Lucille declared. "I asked around and heard the tale. I know your bartender leveled a shotgun at my brother at ten paces." Her voice hiccupped with emotion, and she started to lower her weapon.

Jo hoped Lucille broke down. It would be much easier to comfort her than shoot her. But like a drooping plant suddenly watered, Lucille's gaze focused again on Carter as she stood straight and whipped the gun back toward Jo.

Jo paused. Caution and fear entwined to halt all her surreptitious movements.

"Enough stalling," Lucille said to Carter. "Apologize right now for killing my kin. Or you can watch me kill this adventuress first." She gestured at Jo with the gun. "Perhaps, a shot to her belly for the most pain?"

"Don't," Carter said, firmly, quietly, and seemingly without panic.

For her part, Jo felt dread, along with more than a few drops of terror, begin to slide along her spine. If Carter felt the same way, he hid it behind a face that any card player would be proud of. *Was this really her ignoble end?* All because she'd dared to own a saloon and answer men's need for willing women.

Some days, it just didn't pay to be a capitalist!

Lucille glared straight at Jo, although she seemed to barely see her—her eyes were so glazed with vengeance and fury.

"I don't know what my brother saw in you anyway."

"It might be her lovely ankles," Carter suggested, causing Jo and Lucille both to focus their attention back on him. Jo noted the hopeful look on his face. She nodded, continuing to inch her hand down as quickly as she could.

"Her ankles!" Lucille scoffed.

All Carter had to do was distract the crazy woman and not get himself killed. *Easy.* Hope sang through Jo's veins as she reached all the way beneath her hemline, her fingers curling around the handle of her derringer.

In the same instant, Lucille swung the pistol in Carter's direction and shot him.

Jo jumped at the loud reverberation.

"Carter!" she cried, sparing a glance at him and finding him pinned against his chair by the force of the gun's discharge, eyes closed, and cursing a blue streak. But he was alive!

Palming her derringer, Jo straightened. And then everything seemed to happen as slow as molasses on a cold day.

Lucille's gaze left her victim, and both her face and the gun began to swivel toward Jo.

"The wages of sin are death," the woman said.

Jo briefly hesitated, holding her breath. *Shoot a woman?* It seemed a terrible act, one she'd never considered having to do, but it was clearly shoot or be shot.

Not the head, not the chest. I can't do it! Luckily, the riverboat costume was skimpy enough she could see an long expanse of Lucille's leg.

Jo aimed low and fired. *Pop!* Bright-red blood bloomed low on Lucille's thigh.

"That's for my horse," Jo muttered as Lucille screamed and then screamed again, stumbling sideways and grabbing at the table as she dropped her weapon. Then the brunette crashed heavily to the floor.

Jo jumped up, ignoring Lucille's sobbing and yelling, and paused only to level a kick to the woman's gun, sending it skittering to the other side of the room. Then Jo rounded the table.

Carter!

He was leaning back, looking ashen with pain, clasping his left shoulder with his right hand.

Jo laid a steadying hand on his arm, then sank to her knees by his side to inspect the wound.

"Jameson, honey, I don't think it's too bad."

He blinked at her. "God, I must be dying."

Her stomach lurched. *Had he been shot more than once?*

"No, why do you say that? It looks like merely a shoulder wound." She said "merely" even though seeing his blood, red and oozing, terrified her.

"Because you called me by my first name," he said. "You would never do that unless you thought I was heading for the pearly gates." Then his face broke out in a wincing smile, and she nearly punched his other shoulder.

He grabbed for her with the hand that had been clasping his injury. And despite the blood on his fingers, she let him take her hand and anchor her to him.

"Jameson," she repeated. Then she leaned in and kissed him. In that moment, Candace with Jameson's girls, who'd heard the shots, appeared in the gaming room.

Amidst their gasps and Lucille's groans, Jo murmured against his lips, "We're alive. I had my doubts for a few minutes."

Then she could say nothing more as he kissed her hard, affirming they were indeed very much alive. She wanted to stay right there, her mouth on his and never move an inch.

Eventually, however, he released her.

"Luckily, she's a terrible shot. But you better send one of the ladies to fetch Ben," he advised.

"And a doctor," Jo added.

He nodded and winced as he moved, and she imagined it hurt like hell.

"I'll go." She started to get up.

"No," he said. "You stay right here where I can keep an eye on you. Just having you with me, sweet lady, is the only tonic I'll need. Ever." He emphasized his words by squeezing her hand more tightly

She smiled back at him. "All right. Let me sort things out first."

Reluctantly, Jo rose to her feet and faced the stunned women.

"We had a bit of an issue." She glanced at Lucille, who now lay still with her eyes closed but breathing heavily. "But it's under control now. Christine," Jo addressed Carter's long-time employee, "would you please go get Ben? Do you know where he lives? Can you drive the carriage?"

"Yes, ma'am," she answered and was rushing for the stairs.

"And a doctor, too," Jo called after her. Then she looked at the other ladies. "I think one of you should go with her. Make sure you bring back a doctor."

Another nodded and ran after Christine.

"Can someone get a blanket and pillow for Lucille, but don't move her in case it makes her bleed more," Jo said, already turning her attention back to Jameson, who was watching her admiringly with his fascinating golden-brown eyes. "And a towel for Mr. Carter, quick now."

As someone handed her a clean bar towel which she pressed against his wound, her heart expanded at what his words implied—that he loved her the way she loved him.

EPILOGUE

Jo looked up from the ruby ring glittering between Jameson's pinched fingers, and he decided her eyes, like the finest emeralds, outshone it by far. The words of his nervously delivered proposal were carried away, out into the darkness and over the river. He waited, knowing his heart was going to beat right out of his chest if she didn't speak soon.

His gorgeous lady looked away from him, sending her stunned gaze over the bow of the ship where they stood, and she stared at the last rays of the fiery orange sun sinking gracefully into the Mississippi River.

What the hell was she thinking? He needed to know.

Twice a day, she crossed the river. In the morning, she went over to Keokuk to tend to her business, and sometimes Jameson joined her for an evening on dry land at the new Pork and Swallow, bigger, better, and livelier than the old one.

Clearly, her ladies were happy, Pete was happy, and Jo seemed content. They had a private room fixed up at her saloon, but normally, she crossed the river again, and they spent their nights on his ship.

This had gone on for months, ever since they'd defeated Lucille together. He felt sorry for the woman now. Mercifully, Frank's sister was incarcerated in the Northern Illinois Hospital and Asylum for the Insane, rather than having ended up hanging from the end of a rope. And he thanked his lucky stars once more that she was truly the worst shot he'd ever encountered.

When he'd heard the fire alarm bells peeling again one night, his stomach sank. He'd raced his horse hard and fast across the bridge to Keokuk, only to see an abandoned warehouse burning. Most likely a hobo had tried to cook something and had lost control of the situation. But something changed in Jameson that night.

He'd decided then and there he wanted to make sure she was truly his lady for the rest of their livelong days. After all, he was firmly hers. So he'd gone ring shopping.

Finally, Jo looked at him again, and he thought he saw tears.

"Why?" she asked, her voice barely above a whisper.

He frowned. He hadn't expected such a reaction, nor her question. *Why the hell not?*

She reached up and softly, sweetly stroked his cheek.

"Don't you think it ruins the image of a saloon-owning madam," she asked, "if I'm a lawfully married woman?"

He tamped down the fingers of hurt that curled around his gut at her hesitation and her questioning.

"That's ridiculous. I want you for my own," he insisted.

"I am utterly yours," she promised. "You know that. And I already live with you."

"You could as easily move out," he protested. *Damn!* This wasn't what he'd anticipated. He'd thought she would take the ring, kiss him, and say a resounding yes, and they'd be in their cabin by now with their clothing off. Not debating the benefits and finer points of marriage.

She rolled her eyes. "I could move out anyway, married or not."

Jameson leveled her with a stare that he hoped spoke volumes.

"I'm not planning to," she added quickly, reading his message. "I love our life." She stepped into the circle of his arms and nuzzled his neck.

"And I'll confess right now in case you don't know, Mr. Carter, I love you."

All the air left his lungs. There was only one thing left to say.

"I love you, too. I love you as big as this river."

She laughed, a delightful sexy sound, and he squeezed her tightly under his hands.

"I just want everyone to know you're *my* ladylove."

He bent his head and claimed her lips, softly at first. Then he probed his tongue along the seam of her lips and felt her welcome him inside.

When they eventually separated, Jo took the ring from him and slipped it on her left hand, onto the proper finger right where it belonged. She moved her hand up and down, admiring it.

"I'll flash this ring around, and I'll let everyone know who placed it on my finger," she offered.

"Maybe you'll change your mind about letting me make you my wedded wife," he teased, feeling fairly certain he could. "Maybe I can change it for you tonight."

"Maybe," she allowed, sucking her lower lip in a way that drove him wild with lust. "At least, we'll have fun trying."

When Jo came home from The Pork and Swallow a week later, all the lights were on as usual, which always allowed her to see the boat from her side of the river and to have an easy drive up to the dock when on his side.

However, as she drove closer, she could see two new lamps positioned on the dock, illuminating the starboard hull in front of her.

The Josephine.

Good God! She stared at the rich-red lettering, edged in black.

Jumping down from her carriage seat, she left the horse right where it stood.

"Carter!" she called as she flew toward the gangplank, delight and astonishment vying for supremacy in her breast.

"Right here," he said, stopping her in her tracks. He'd been standing dockside in the shadows, apparently to watch her reaction.

"You named her after me?" The gesture touched her in a place where only Carter's love ever could. She rushed up to him, throwing her arms around him.

A big, unwieldy riverboat shared her name! It was the most glorious thing anyone had ever done for her.

"Is that all right?" he asked, taking her in his arms.

She heard the caution in his voice. *How adorable!* He wasn't sure of himself. *Was it all right?* Yes, it was. A sense of belonging encircled her heart securely. Suddenly, this floating riverboat seemed solid and permanent. *This was home!*

She supposed she would have to let him marry her after all. Winding her arms around his neck, she breathed in the familiar bay rum scent of her man. Loving it, loving him.

"Do I have to emblazon your name on the side of my saloon, too?" she teased, arching an eyebrow at him.

He laughed. "Only if it brings in more customers."

She cocked her head. "More likely, it will scare them away."

"Be nice, Jo," he said, holding her tightly.

"You didn't fall for me because I was nice," she pointed out.

"True." He bent his head and nibbled her neck until she yelped. "But I did fall for you and hard. And now you're my riverboat queen."

A riverboat queen? She quite liked that.

"All right then," she said. "Let's board *The Josephine*."

"Oh, I intend to," he said, scooping her into his arms and waggling his eyebrows with wicked intent, while she dissolved into peals of laughter. "That's an absolutely safe bet."

Finis

DEFIANT HEARTS

AN INTRIGUING PROPOSITION
Defiant Hearts Prequel

Insidious blackmail, the threat of foreclosure, and a fake engagement—all in one week! Elise is a lady in distress, and Michael is the man to help her in this fast-paced carriage ride romance through the streets of Victorian Boston.

AN IMPROPER SITUATION
Defiant Hearts Book 1

A stranger arrives from Boston seeking Miss Charlotte Sanborn. What Reed finds is an irresistible spinster. Before long, Charlotte is riding a train heading east toward high society, delicious romance, and perilous intrigue in *An Improper Situation*.

AN IRRESISTIBLE TEMPTATION
Defiant Hearts Book 2

Gifted pianist, Sophie Malloy flees Boston with a broken heart and meets a dusty cowboy. Sparks fly! But Riley's future is in Colorado while her career takes her to San Francisco. Is it love or merely *An Irresistible Temptation?*

AN INESCAPABLE ATTRACTION
Defiant Hearts Book 3

With heartache haunting her and a murderous gambler on her trail, Eliza has no choice but to run. Thaddeus will do anything—even kill—to protect the only woman he's ever loved. Peril is merely a hoofbeat behind in *Inescapable Attraction*.

AN INCONCEIVABLE DECEPTION
Defiant Hearts Book 4

Boston society girl Rose Malloy has everything including a loving fiancé. Then her past resurfaces bringing heartbreak, lies, intrigue, and murder in *An Inconceivable Deception*.

AN IMPASSIONED REDEMPTION
Defiant Hearts Novella

Take one sinfully handsome riverboat gambler, add a gorgeous saloon madam, and stir them up with murderous foul play and sizzling romance. Jameson plays to win, and he intends to win the heart of Josephine, in *An Impassioned Redemption*.

ABOUT THE AUTHOR

USA Today bestselling author Sydney Jane Baily writes historical romance set in Victorian England, late 19th-century America, the Middle Ages, the Georgian era, and the Regency period. She believes in happily-ever-after stories with engaging characters and attention to period detail.

Born and raised in California, she has traveled the world, spending a lot of exceedingly happy time in the U.K. where her extended family resides, eating fish and chips, drinking shandies, and snacking on Maltesers and Cadbury bars. Sydney currently lives in New England with her family—human, canine, and feline.

You can learn more about her books, read her blog, sign up for her newsletter (and get a free book), and contact her via her website at SydneyJaneBaily.com. She loves to hear from her readers.

www.ingramcontent.com/pod-product-compliance
Lightning Source LLC
Chambersburg PA
CBHW031031190726
48286CB00003BA/1113